I Have a Theory about That

Judy Balan is a novelist and practising psychological astrologer, completing a postgraduate diploma in Jungian studies (depth psychology) with the Society for Psychology and Healing (SOPH), UK. *I Have a Theory about That* is her sixth novel. Judy can be contacted at balan.judy@gmail.com.

I Have a Theory about That

JUDY BALAN

hachette
INDIA

First published in 2019 by Hachette India
(Registered name: Hachette Book Publishing India Pvt. Ltd)
An Hachette UK company
www.hachetteindia.com

SRD

ISBN 978-93-5195-072-1

Hachette Book Publishing India Pvt. Ltd
4th & 5th Floors, Corporate Centre,
Plot No. 94, Sector 44, Gurugram 122003, India

Typeset in Joanna MT Std 11/14.5
by R Ajith Kumar, New Delhi

Printed and bound in India
by Manipal Technologies Limited, Manipal

MIX
Paper from
responsible sources
FSC™ C043100

For subpersonalities, yours and mine

A year to find love

This is the story of Meghana and Tania. Two young-ish women on a quest for love. *Real love*, they say, like love has a single definition. Both women were born exactly on the cusp of the millennial generation, and are understandably confused about life. Add being desi and, more specifically, being from Chennai to that mix, you have an assortment of the most contradictory values that make holding it all together in one personality an extraordinary psychological challenge. It's a good thing that self-awareness isn't one of their strong suits.

But that's where the similarity ends. Meg – as she prefers to be known because 'no one has time for three syllables' – is a fan of the concrete world. Things she can touch, see, smell, taste and more importantly, *explain*. Meg needs everything to have a purpose. It's why she chose advertising over art. You can be creative without being an entitled brat who can't hold down a job. Artists – they walk around all tortured like the world owes them a living. It doesn't. You have creative energy? Put it to use by building a brand, where there are always clear objectives, strategies, results and *a salary*. A hard-earned salary. It's secure, stable and responsible. It is what adults do.

It's precisely this responsible adult vibe that draws the happy-go-lucky-take-each-day-as-it-comes opposites into her life. But that's all right, that can be fixed. Meg is an excellent fixer. And this year, she is fixing her love life. In fact, she's already taken the first step by breaking up with Neel, her boyfriend of four years and polar opposite. Poor Neel. Being at the receiving end of Meg's cool, surgical precision when severing a relationship is not fun. And if Meg is dealing with feelings of her own, she's only dimly aware of it. Twenty-nine years of repressing feelings can do that to a person.

But Meg is convinced she made the right move. Neel is too much of a go-with-the-flow type of guy, a musician waiting for his big break (the horror!). Meg, as we've established, is the kind of woman who likes to have a goal and *work* towards it. And the Goal was a solid partnership that she could count on, which would most likely take the form of marriage in about a couple of years, a nice house and a low-maintenance pet. But that was nowhere in sight and with Meg being Meg, the breakup was inevitable. It was all very sad, but she's more determined than ever to find this love. She even has a six-month action plan chalked out with spreadsheets and everything.

Now, this is something that Tania finds not only uninspiring but downright absurd. Tania, unlike Meg, has been in and out of love since she was 17, but a big part of her relationship pattern has been a tendency to find unavailable, commitment-phobic or pathological liars for partners. A trajectory that may have crushed the average person's faith in romantic love – but not Tania's. She has always maintained that she has no regrets as far as her emotional decisions are concerned since each one of those relationships that went down the drain brought her so much closer to an understanding of herself. But 12 years of consistent disappointment can be a bit much even for someone like Tania, who is now quite ready to get it right this time. A big part of Tania's idea of real love is the emotional fulfilment that comes with it. That inner sense of something that *feels* right. And since emotions do not behave rationally, how can you ever hope to find love using spreadsheets? Certainty and love are mutually exclusive. If you want guarantees, go buy a microwave. But if you're sure you want love, you'll have to do this scary thing called trusting the process. *Surrender*. Allow yourself to be led by something bigger than yourself. Pay attention to synchronicities, serendipities, dreams and little signs from the universe. After you've set your intention, of course. That's all that matters. Wanting something badly enough and aligning yourself to its vibration (whatever that means). That's the only way, as her recent half-baked dabbling in random western and eastern esoteric philosophics has confirmed. If only she had known all this a decade ago…oh, wait! That's not how it works. Everything has been unfolding according to the mysterious, infinitely wise plan of the universe. Now that Tania's consciously cooperating with it, there is no reason why this shouldn't happen for her this year. After all, if Meg can have enough confidence in her spreadsheets to challenge her beliefs, how much more trust should she have in the universe? So, challenge accepted.

By the end of the year – their 29th year – one or both women will prove their theories right. Or wrong. Oh, and these two neurotics live together.

Fun.

1

'Advertising is simply art that has direction and purpose. I like to apply the same logic to emotions in my quest for love.' – Meg

It's Monday. Meg's favourite day of the week. It gives her a sense of purpose. Of feeling alive. A clear direction for her Type A compulsions, unlike weekends when there is all this pressure to relax and have fun. 'Relaxation is overrated,' she was once quoted by a very frustrated masseuse who couldn't get her to close her eyes and stop making verbal to-do lists. But this Monday is different. Special. Today, she will initiate Operation Love in One Year. This means a whole new space for her intense drive and focus to go wild in. Oh, what would Meg do in a world where there was nothing to prove?

Meg stirs from her sleep just seconds before her alarm goes off. It's loud enough to wake up the neighbours with the most annoying song of the 1980s: 'Wake Me up before You Go-Go.' It rings much longer than alarms are meant to because of Meg's peculiar nightly ritual – hiding the alarm in a new place every night. Her logic is, she'd be in such a hurry to get out of bed and stop the song that grated on an entire generation for years that she'd be fully awake in the process.

She finds it inside one of her old handbags and puts it out of its misery. 'Now I'm definitely awake,' she says, stretching on her way into the bathroom. There is nothing glamorous about this bathroom except for a very old bathtub that Meg barely ever uses. (Theory #2236: Bathtubs are for the unambitious. Driven people only have time for a shower.) Lemon yellow tiles that Meg hates (whatever happened to good, old-fashioned white tiles or grey tiles? Who needs their bathroom to remind them of lemonade?), a standard mirror and sink, a shower and attached toilet. That's what you get at a rent of ₹30,000 in a nice residential street in Alwarpet. No frills, none. The rent is the frill. And yet, there is something about this bathroom that makes you want to hang out there and maybe read a magazine. It's the Meg magic. Spotless, completely dry and always smelling like freshly baked chocolate and cinnamon cake. Is it weird to have your bathroom smell of cake? Definitely. But that's Meg for you. Her brain is clearly divided into 'Okay' and 'Not Okay' sections, and chocolate cake and bathroom made it into 'Okay' and lemonade didn't – and there is nothing you or the rest of the world can do about it. She brushes, showers, gets into her work clothes – a pair of neatly ironed black trousers, grey silk blouse and a magenta scarf all laid out on the bed the previous night – and distractedly runs her fingers through her naturally straight and silky collar-bone-length black hair that, according to Tania, she 'totally takes for granted' and mentally goes over her day's to-do list in less than 30 minutes. Meg takes a quick peek into her flatmate's room to say goodbye, but Tania is meditating with that creepy ambient music that makes Meg extremely uncomfortable. She'll just have to catch up with her in the evening.

~

It's a busy day at Red Dot Digital, the digital advertising agency where Meg is the creative director on paper but where, on an average day, she juggles multiple roles including HR, admin head, client whisperer, English teacher and the right hand and frontal lobe of the big boss, Shawn Thomas D'Souza whom they all fondly refer to as STD. It's no surprise then that Meg loves her job. It feeds her need to feel useful – like nothing would run without her.

'Meg! There you are!' Nitin, the account manager, comes up to her, looking like something out of a spy novel. 'Need to talk,' he whispers discreetly when he gets close enough.

That's the other thing Meg has always loved about advertising: the daily drama. It satisfies her craving for excitement, without compromising her need for stability and security. Meg already knows what this is about – it's what it always is. A client is about to explode and the client servicing head isn't happy, and this is about to have a domino effect on the rest of the agency – everyone's going to be in a bit of a mood until she, the fixer, fixes the situation one way or the other. It's like being the star of her own adventure series.

'Why all the mystery, Nitin?' she follows Nitin to the conference room as he furiously hushes her. 'We don't want to alarm anyone,' he says.

'Alarm anyone?' Meg says, amused, as they enter the room. 'Fine, I'll play along,' she says as she pulls a chair and makes herself comfortable. 'Is it aliens? Does Major William Cage need our help?' she says mockingly.

'It's Warner & Parker,' Nitin says with a deadpan expression.

'What about Warner & Parker?'

'Well, there are rumours flying around about a merger. Actually, I heard it myself. Muthu was discussing it with someone on a call.' Muthu is the head of the accounting department.

Meg rolls her eyes. 'Those rumours have been flying around for years, Nitin. STD has been talking about the Warner & Parker merger since I got here five years ago!'

'But Muthu…'

'It could be anything. Maybe he was only using it as a reference. You have no context. And besides, why is that so frightening?'

'Because,' Nitin finally takes a seat. 'I actually like it here. After all these years hopping from agency to agency across cities, I finally like this place. I like my life here! In this city, in this agency…I like the people – I even like you, though you're annoying as fuck but you're an excellent buffer between STD and the rest of us.'

'Thank you,' Meg says. 'I don't know what I'd do without friends like you.'

'I'm serious. I don't want to move, and god knows what's going to happen if the management changes. We've just had a baby, Meg! I'm responsible for a tiny human life!' Meg stops him. Nitin is usually unflustered – now Meg is beginning to worry.

'Hey,' Meg extends her arm to comfort him, but she can't reach him. 'Too far, sorry.'

He laughs nervously.

'Listen,' Meg says seriously. 'It's not going to happen and if it is, I'll be the first to know…'

'And I'll be the first to know after, right?'

'Of course. Now get back to work and torturing the creative team like you normally do.'

Nitin leaves, somewhat comforted but Meg feels a sharp sensation in the pit of her stomach. After all, she is returning to work after a week (unheard of in Meg's work history) but she had been running an insanely high temperature, and Tania had confiscated her phone. What if STD had called? Her phone had been switched off. But STD has been very spaced out ever since his divorce and even more erratic than usual. Meg tells herself not to panic. But the truth is, she really likes it here too, and if there was ever a time that she'd be grateful for things to remain exactly as they are, it would be now. She really means business when she says she wants to find love in a year. But that isn't possible if the most stable part of her existence is unravelling.

'It's just a stupid feeling,' Meg dismisses her instincts like she normally does. 'Doesn't mean anything. There are zero facts to back it up.' She has better things to do, like finding the love of her life, than wasting time on pointless speculation. She reaches for her Filofax, the way some people reach for Nutella when stressed, and begins to write.

This *Week's* To-do:

- *Accept more invitations to social events and once there, mingle*
- *Open mind to swiping right*
- *Remember that only the end result matters, not how you get there*
- *Take Nitin's advice: send out 'single vibes' by developing a 'more approachable persona'*

Uhh, no. Scratch that last one. What does that even mean?

2

'Never underestimate the power of intention.' – Tania

Tania is seated on the floor, legs folded, palms open, back straight, strikingly light brown eyes closed, her waist-length hair falling in messy waves. Tania is mostly satisfied with the way she looks except for her untamed, frizzy hair that she not-so-fondly calls Eddie (as in Eddie Van Halen). There's a half-drunk mug of green tea at her side. She's taken the day off to meditate, detox and set intentions. The perks of running your own business. Sort of. Also, not her own, she runs it with her long-time friend Aditi. This is apart from being a freelance artist. It turned a year old just a week ago, in fact. The business, that is. Wedding planning. It's the new cupcake baking, and neither Tania nor Aditi were particularly serious when they started out – they were just doing it for the joy of it. But a year later, they've done well enough to want more. In fact, they're on a shortlist of wedding planners for a mid-sized city celebrity, the modern-classical dancer Meera Anand. Of course, they don't know this just yet or Tania would be too excited to get herself into a meditative state of mind. Not that a meditative state is at all easy to achieve when you live in a flat sandwiched between Mrs Sitaram aka Meenakshi Aunty who lives on the fourth floor and Nandini aka Nandu who lives on the second and does not like being called 'Aunty' – two ladies who are much too invested in Meg and Tania's lives and are both currently rooting for Tania to win the bet against Meg (since Meg has zero tolerance for 'Indian Aunty Intrusion' and Tania finds it all 'quite sweet actually') from their respective balconies.

'I am telling you... Tania will win. So fair, so tall, big eyes...' Meenakshi Aunty is yelling at Nandu in the background.

'Yes! In fact, I know a very good boy...engineer...very modern...does not mind if she is not Hindu...he'll be so correct for her, you know?'

'How nice! She's a nice girl. I hope she finds someone soon. Not like that other one. Meghana. Such an arrogant girl.'

Tania grunts and rises from the floor and marches to her balcony. This isn't the first time the two are having what is clearly a very personal discussion from across their balconies, but this is the first time they're discussing her and Meg! 'Can you both get a phone or something? I can hear you! And so can everyone else in the building!'

'Oh good, good! Now, tell me if you want to meet the boy!' Nandu sounds delighted to play matchmaker.

'No, Nandu. I'm not meeting *any* boy. That is not how this works. I mean, thank you for your concern and all, but I really shouldn't have told you about the bet.' Tania lets her annoyance show for once. Maybe Meg is right about Indian aunties after all.

'Oh, okay then,' Meenakshi Aunty sulks. 'We only want you to win.'

Tania sighs and decides not to upset the neighbours again. Especially since Nandu is their landlady as well. 'I'm sorry,' she says. 'I didn't mean to be rude – I know you are both very fond of me. But you have to stop talking about me from the balcony! Plus, I'm trying to meditate, and I can't focus.'

Meenakshi Aunty smiles fondly. 'Okay, okay. Promise. We will talk on the phone only about you,' she says sincerely.

Tania sighs again as she returns to her meditation. If Meg knew, she'd be furious. 'They have no boundaries!' she always complains. 'Only in India!' Tania had always called it 'Eastern warmth' – it's something she's always been proud of compared to the complete lack of neighbourliness in the UK where much of her family lives, but she's beginning to see Meg's point. She settles on the floor, turns on the music and relaxes her way into her centre again.

After about half an hour, Tania opens her eyes in slo-mo as if surfacing from an alternate dimension. She rises gracefully, but stubs her toe against the bed the minute she puts one foot before the other. She's tall – 5'8" – has great skin (clearly the detoxes are paying off) and bears a striking resemblance to Monica Bellucci of the early 2000s. A messier, clumsier version that is. She opens her closet and tries to remember where she put her Rider Waite tarot deck. One peek into the closet and you'd understand why. There aren't any clothes in this one. Just tarot and oracle decks. Some crystals. Sage. Books on alternative healing modalities. Scented candles. And little bottles containing god alone knows what. It's like something out of Snape's storeroom but weirder.

'Ah, there you are,' she pulls out her beloved Rider Waite deck and talks to it like it's a small, furry animal. 'You and I need to talk.'

She grabs a couple of crystals, lights a scented candle and sits down again, deck in hand. She's now about to set her intentions for the Cancer new moon. Astrology is her new toy, one that's consumed her more than any of her other New Age interests.

There is much to learn, and astrology can be dangerous in the hands of a novice though Tania is blissfully unaware of this at this point. She also does not think of herself as a novice, thank you very much. The Cancer new moon it is. New moons are supposed to be the beginning of a new cycle, and all Tania knows is that this new moon falls close to where her sun is (in Cancer) and therefore, it has special significance for her. That's why all the extra rituals this morning. She closes her eyes and starts to shuffle the cards, concentrating on her question: *What intention should I focus on?*

Yep, one New Age practice to assist another New Age practice. After what seems like a ridiculously long time shuffling the deck to 'clear the energies', Tania is ready to pull her cards. It's the Fool. The first card of the major arcana with the image of a merry young man about to leap off a cliff except he doesn't know that yet. He can't see that he's at the precipice. Not a very inspiring picture, but Tania is smiling. If you asked, she'd tell you that the Fool only pops up when one is beginning a grand quest in some area of their lives. He appears at that moment when you sense new possibilities bubbling within though you're not quite in a new place yet. She takes that as a nod from the universe to go ahead and set her intentions to find love this year.

Before you write this off as New Age mumbo-jumbo, Tania would have you know that the ancients used moon cycles as timing devices and planned almost their whole lives around it. And check it out – they conquered worlds, raised large families, managed livestock, built cities and entire civilizations while the rationally oriented modern man considers it an achievement if he can go a whole day on the Internet without getting distracted by cute animal memes, all the while scoffing at ancient traditions he knows nothing about. So, mock her all you want but she's betting on the ancients on this one. She knows the difference between a new moon, crescent, first quarter, gibbous, full moon and on and on and better still, she's learning how to use them – something Meg likes to call 'loola'.

And Tania would have you know something about Meg too. Many moons ago (forgive the pun!) when Meg was 21, twice as ambitious and half as emotionally intelligent, she was in a relationship with a guy for three years, a year of which he was busy hooking up with Tania. Meg didn't notice anything because of 'work'. And no, Tania didn't know either. But this is the story of how they first met: when they found out and bonded over their mutual loathing of Kunal. And that's pretty much all they still have in common though for some unfathomable reason, they've remained close friends and even shared a flat for five years.

Also, Meg is the one who's loola, insisting that people call her Meg as opposed to Meghana because 'nobody should waste time on trisyllabic names when a monosyllabic alternative like Meg is right there for the taking. Really, who says things like that? Poor kid, Tania would say with the empathy of someone who has seen Meg's natal chart: 'She's got Mars in her first house in Capricorn, making her feel like the world won't run without her mojo. She's driven by a compulsive need to not waste time. Annoying as that is, it's clearly not her fault.'

This, of course, does not mean that Tania isn't competitive herself. She's very much looking forward to proving her theory right. Though Meg might be more interested in proving Tania wrong (a charming Mercury in Virgo trait).

Tania carefully wraps her tarot deck, crystals and sage in a velvet cloth, places them back in the closet and moves on to her next ritual – an intention journal – reserved only for special cosmic events.

Intentions for the Cancer new moon

- Release toxic exes and all extra baggage in order to make room for healthy new relationship
- Find the love of my life, someone who instinctively feels like family
- Learn to draw boundaries and ward off energy vampires
- Develop intuitive gifts to know what steps to take (and not to take) in the quest for love
- Replace clingy love with self-love

3

'Newton's first law states that a body at rest will remain at rest and a body in motion will remain in motion unless it is acted upon by an external force. I have decided to be the external force!' – Meg

'Since when are you interested in baby showers, Meghana Rao?' Tania tries to balance the handmade props and games she's organized for Preity's baby shower. Preity is a mutual friend – well, Tania's friend and by extension, Meg's.

'I was invited,' Meg shrugs with her back to Tania so she can't look at her face and divine her master plan.

'You're always invited,' Tania says. 'This is the first time I've actually seen you enthusiastic about going. What's going on?' Meg has habitually declined party invitations for years, especially ones that involve groups of cackling women. Meg has tried, but she has never quite managed to get the whole sisterhood thing right. As opposed to Tania who has had some of the most solid female friendships a girl could hope for. Meg blames this on her critical, unaffectionate mother who has clearly deprived her of a nurturing bone. But tonight is different. Meg has a plan. And when Meg has a goal to work towards, she gets behind it with the focus and tenacity of a mountain goat. Undeterred even by her fear of ladies' nights.

'Nothing… I just feel like company. But maybe you're right. I'll regret coming five minutes into the party.'

'Noooo!' Tania calls out from her room predictably, and Meg smiles like the sinister strategist that she is. 'I like the new Meg! If…that's what this is…just quickly get dressed before you change your mind.'

'Okay!' Meg merrily opens her 'girly drawer' which has exactly two sets of clothes for occasions like this: flowy and floral. Also, not black. Conventionally feminine is the look of the evening. She decides to go with the mint green dress with tiny white flowers that Tania always says brings out the softness of her features and buffers her sharp jawline which Meg just happens to like. It's all part of the master plan.

'Also, speaking of changing your mind, any news from Neel?' Tania calls out.

'Nope.'

'Maybe you should call and check in on him?'

'Nope.'

'Are we still not discussing Neel?'

'Yup.'

~

'Here. You brought this,' Tania hands Meg a neatly packed gift as they stand outside Preity's door, about to ring the bell.

'Crap, thank you! I'd completely forgotten.'

'I know. That's why I picked it up when I got mine.'

'You're a lifesaver. But wait…you didn't know I was going to this!'

'Yes, but you were invited,' Tania says. 'It's rude not to send a gift.'

Meg is shocked by this revelation. 'You mean you've been carrying gifts from me to all the parties all these years?'

'Of course,' Tania says. 'My friends already think you're weird and I'm the New Ager. Wouldn't want them to think you're rude too.'

'Uhh, first, nobody expects you to send a gift to a birthday party you did not attend…'

'And you'd know because you're such a social animal?'

The door opens while Meg and Tania are busy bickering over party etiquette. Suchi, the co-hostess of the shower is standing there. The other hostess being Tania, of course.

'Well…hi…you both!' You can tell Suchi is clearly surprised to see Meg. 'Meg! How nice of you to come! You look lovely.' Suchi's emotional responses are usually immediately visible in her facial expressions, and so this is quite amusing for anyone watching.

Meg only smiles in response. *I love being unpredictable*, she thinks. *It's so nice when people freeze at the sight of you at their door.*

'Sorry, come in. Here, let me get that.' Suchi makes way for Meg and helps Tania with her props.

They enter what looks like the inside of a designer furniture catalogue, and Tania is surprised to find Meg blending in and even trying to make small talk with the women – most of them moms. Whenever Meg attends parties, she usually heads straight for the bar and then finds the corner that offers the best view so she can stand back and entertain herself with snarky commentary. *Something is definitely going on*, Tania thinks.

But the shower goes on and Meg is an eager participant in all the baby games, mingling, chit-chatting and by the end of the evening, the audience is so charmed that Suchi and Preity want to set her up with a friend of theirs.

'I did ask you first, Tania,' Suchi says.

'You know I don't do set-ups,' Tania says. 'But Meg, since when do you?' Tania is a little irritated – that a) she was not the first to know about Meg's plan and b) that she used the party to be set up – and it shows.

'Are you nervous that I'm going to win?' Meg says while Tania furiously glares at her to shut up. She does not want some of her judgy friends at the party to know about their bet.

'Win? Win what?' Preity wants to know.

'Tell her, Tania,' Meg is feeling cocky.

Tania reluctantly enlightens the group about their little bet. To her surprise and annoyance, everyone seems to be taking Meg's side. 'Sure, you must trust in the universe, but you also have to take action…' and 'Yes, Tania, but what are you doing about finding love? It's not like "The One" is going to magically knock on your door with the missing piece of your soul!' These are supposed to be her friends! How could they not get her at all? Also, Meg. That sneaky little wretch. She'd always known that competition made Meg do crazy things, but she's mad at her nonetheless.

Meg, sensing Tania's shift in mood, steers the conversation back to baby matters and before they know it, the cacklers have completely forgotten the bet.

It's almost 9 p.m. as they leave, and Meg suddenly remembers that she'd promised to have dinner with her mum at 7 p.m. 'Crap!' she mutters.

'What' Tania asks, though she's been giving Meg the silent treatment for the last hour.

'I was supposed to have dinner with my mother today!'

'Ooh, fun. Meg is late for dinner with future Meg.'

'I am nothing like her…' Meg decides not to fall for Tania needling her. She's in an understandably foul mood. 'Never mind. I'd better call her… Hi Ma…'

'You're not coming. I already know.'

'No, no, I am coming. I'm just running late,' Meg says to her own surprise. She had planned on cancelling, but her mother has a way of turning her back into the 10-year-old child who hadn't done her homework. It's almost funny watching Meg, a grown woman and self-assured boss lady morph into a blithering idiot with her mother.

'When?' Her mother's tone is sharp and her accent even sharper.

'Be there in 10 minutes.' Meg hangs up but from the look on her face you can tell that her mother is her boggart. It's almost comical.

'I can come with you if you want,' Tania offers generously.

'Why? You don't even like her.' Meg is suspicious. Tania usually has to be coaxed and bribed into any kind of interaction with Meg's mother.

'Uhh, can you blame me? I just thought maybe I could act as a buffer since you've *already* really pissed her off… Never mind.'

'No, no! I love that idea. Thank you! Please come with me!' Meg is desperate, and Tania loves it.

~

It takes longer than 10 minutes to reach T. Nagar where her mother lives, near the aesthetic nightmare that is Pondy Bazaar. Thankfully, they've painted the building exteriors recently making them a little less hard on the eyes. Growing up in this part of Chennai is why Meg constantly fantasized about luxury interiors and designer furniture as a child. But value-for-money middle-class Tamilian roots are hard to shake off, as Meg has demonstrated in many little ways from her habit of collecting plastic covers (so useful!) to diluting the dishwashing liquid (it's all a ruse, nobody needs soap to be that strong!) to only ordering pizzas on Wednesdays when there is an offer running (no one should pay full price for food that's basically junk), even while consciously cutting herself off from her cultural roots.

Meg drums her fingers nervously against the elevator wall. She notices that the ugly grill gates are still as creaky as when she was growing up, and the elevator still wobbles like it might collapse any minute. 'Third floor,' the grating intercom voice announces.

'You ready?' Tania asks as they stand outside apartment number 38C, which is really more of a 32B.

'Yup,' Meg says, ringing the bell.

Her mother takes a whole minute to get to the door. 'Oh, you really came,' she says, her face deadpan. Meg is the spitting image of her mother. Kavitha Rao is an older, way more uptight Meg. She's dressed in a nice kurta but with a mismatched salwar, her long hair is in a neat bun, and would be deemed too young to be Meg's mother if not for the authoritative voice that gave you the feeling that you'd entered the principal's office.

'Hello, Aunty,' Tania flashes her a wholesome smile like there is no static at all in the air.

'Come in,' is all Kavitha says, and Meg and Tania make their way into the living room, which, according to Meg, is anything but liveable. For starters, there is still the '80s showcase right in the middle of the house, which as Meg puts it, is a large, ugly piece of furniture with a collection of tiny figurines, ashtrays, random souvenirs, little dolls and just about every tacky thing you can collect, that no one needs displayed on glass shelves. This showcase is flanked by two single wooden sofas, which belong to a larger three-piece wooden sofa set, with a rectangular wooden teapoy in the middle. Things are exactly as they were in 1989 when Meg was fantasizing about wooden floors, yellow lighting, non-wooden furniture and bathtubs and refrigerators that didn't come in copper-sulphate blue.

'Have you had dinner?' Kavitha asks as they sit down.

'Yeah…' Meg says slowly trying to assess her mother's reaction. 'But you know what, we can have another dinner if you've made it…'

'No, it's fine.'

They sit quietly for a few seconds. 'Would you like some Rasna?'

Ah, more fond memories. 'Yes, Aunty, I'd love some Rasna,' Tania says. She had no idea it was still in the market.

'So, you were working late, is it?' Kavitha asks as she looks for a pair of guest glasses – anything not made of steel, that is.

'Uh, actually, we had to go to this friends' shower and I forgot…'

'Shower *aa*?'

'Baby shower,' Meg says. 'It's a kind of a party for an expectant mother.'

'I know what a baby shower is. You think I'm so ignorant or what?'

Meg takes a deep breath and takes the Rasna from her mother. Tania and Meg sip the Rasna in strained silence as Kavitha watches them from across the room.

'Very nice Rasna, Aunty,' Tania tries to play her promised part of the buffer.

'So, you broke up with Neel.' Kavitha says, causing both Meg and Tania to choke on their drinks. How on *earth* could she have possibly known that!

'How did you even…'

'I am your mother. I know everything,' is the simple answer.

'I normally don't like to put pressure on you to get married and all. But you have to think about your age also. And stop being so fussy.'

Meg is shocked. She had expected some general berating of her lifestyle from her mother mostly in the realm of financial decisions and of course, a lecture for showing up late. But marriage? No. Since her own marriage hadn't gone so spectacularly, Kavitha rarely expressed any urgency in Meg 'settling down'. She did, however, maintain the outward appearance of a conventional life as illustrated by the framed photo of her and Meg's father looking very much in love, sitting pretty inside the showcase. Surprisingly Kavitha Rao was once known for her adventurous streak. She and Meg's father had met in college and eloped five years later because her family wouldn't hear of a 'love marriage'.

Meg's father, as it turned out, had a far more intense adventurous streak and abandoned his family when Meg was only a baby to pursue painting and photography. Nothing ever came of his art and he used to return promptly every few months to borrow money from his wife to pay the bills while he focused on achieving greatness. He eventually disappeared, but making peace with her family – her only real support system – had turned out to be more exhausting than being a single, working mother for Kavitha. And now to think that her own daughter was about to put her in the same position again by going against her family and choosing who she would marry.

'Ma, you didn't even like Neel!' Meg is too caught off guard to say anything else.

'Yes, but at least he was a man.'

'Uhh, as opposed to what?'

'You don't have to keep pretending. You both are lesbians, no?'

After a couple of seconds' silence, Tania bursts out laughing but Meg is still frozen from the turn this evening has taken.

'We wish, Aunty!' Tania says. 'That would've made things so simple.' But Kavitha is not amused. 'In fact,' Tania has a bright idea. 'It's a good thing you brought this up because Meg is very focused on settling down right now and would very much like it if you arranged for her to meet some good Reddy boys.'

'We are *not* Reddys. In fact, we are not even Telugus, Meg's father was a Telugu.' Kavitha retorts out of habit before realizing what Tania has just said.

Meg tries desperately to make eye contact with Tania, to ask what the hell she's doing, but Tania conveniently does not look at her.

'Is this true?' Kavitha asks Meg, who is really caught between the devil and the deep sea. On the one hand, the last thing she wants is for her mother to think she's a lesbian at a time when she's trying to find The One. It would totally sabotage her master plan. But the thought of going the arranged marriage route just to get her mom off her back is too insulting.

'Yes,' Meg finally says. 'But I'm not promising anything.'

And just like that, Kavitha goes from angry crone to doting mother. 'Of course, of course. *Happa*, I am so relieved! I don't have to go explaining your modern relationship complications to my sisters. If I can only arrange your marriage...it will shut a lot of mouths!'

'Ma, I am only agreeing to meet the guy – that's it. The rest depends.'

'Yes, yes, I know. That's enough for now.' Kavitha smiles and fondly touches her daughter's cheek. It's a bit much for Meg to handle in one evening so they quickly leave, Kavitha waving goodbye from the balcony.

'What the hell?' Meg says as soon as they're out of earshot.

'Revenge is sweet,' Tania smiles. 'You really shouldn't have been such a manipulative bitch at the shower today.'

'You know, you actually did me a favour.' Meg points out. 'You just opened up a whole new avenue that I hadn't even considered. It fits right into my master plan.'

'It is tragic how you equate finding love with desperation.'

And they take loving digs at each other all the way home.

4

'Find your centre before you find The One.' – Tania

It's 10 a.m. and Tania is already burning sage. It's been quite difficult to source the herb in Chennai, and she only brings it out when she's in a seriously difficult situation. You see, the Native Americans always burnt sage to clear away negative energies and cleanse the environment in what was called a smudging ceremony, and that's what Tania is doing.

'It's only 10 in the morning!' Meg coughs her way into the living room. 'Who has put you in this loola state with their negative juju already?'

Tania seems very anxious. 'I know that something is up.'

'Like ghosts?' Meg asks.

'Be serious,' Tania snaps as she takes the sage into every nook and cranny of the house.

'You're the one *saging* the house to drive out demons and I need to be serious?'

'I've not got paid for the work I did more than six months ago. It sucks being a freelance artist or a freelance anything in this country! I am so tired of asking for my due! They make me feel bad about asking to be paid for work that I've done!'

'I know. That's why I have a day job,' Meg says like the sensitive, supportive friend that she is.

'Thanks. At least I know I have you to comfort me after.'

'Hey! You know I don't do comfort, I do solutions. You knew that freelance life would be like this! Besides, if people don't pay you, you have to do whatever it takes to get your money! Name them, warn people about them – that's what social media is for. And never take on work without a 100 per cent advance.' Meg cannot help herself from trying to fix other people's problems.

'I can't do that. I can't stoop to their level,' Tania says, putting the sage out at last. 'It's just that all this money that was supposed to have come in would have let me buy the iPad that I need. It's so damn frustrating!'

'Just call, yell at them and tell them you're going to take them down on social media if you do not receive the payment by the end of the week.'

Tania sighs heavily.

'What, you're not going to do it?' Meg says.

'I know this is difficult for you to understand but sometimes, the best way through a frustrating situation is to just do nothing and find your centre. And once you're calm on the inside, things start working themselves out on the outside.' Tania is trying to talk herself out of doing anything rash. She's really quite upset about not being able to buy her tablet.

'Right. The same logic you apply to your love life. Good. At least I don't have to go to ridiculous lengths to beat you at this stupid bet.' Meg gets up to leave for work. 'Oh, and don't wait up for me tonight. I have a date,' she smiles. 'You know, 'cause I'm taking action and moving forward.' Her lips curl in that irritating fashion they always do when she's trying to make a point, and Tania can't wait for her and her perfect hair to get out.

Once Meg leaves, Tania shuts herself in her room and starts to cry. She had meant to scream but her anger always manifests in tears. It's embarrassing, it makes her feel so…impotent. And before she knows it, she finds herself neck deep in almost-thirty doubt and anxiety.

What if every single thing she's believed in so far is a lie? What if Meg is right? She has no money, no relationship, no prospects and is clinging to beliefs that may have just been made up by some hippie in a drug haze. Sure, Meg is the last person on this planet who can be called 'put together', but at least she has money. Tania had always believed in doing everything from the heart. Being authentic. But where has that got her? To think that she could just end up wasting more opportunities because of her beliefs!

Maybe she should do what everyone else has been saying. Maybe she should start directing her actions in a focused manner. Like Meg. Except the very thought of going on a planned date with someone makes her nauseous. But what if that's the only way? Maybe she should make some changes. She just might find that a day job isn't all that bad. Right now, she can't even seem to get the money that's due to her, can't get herself the tablet that she really needs for work, forget about travel or saving for retirement. She simply cannot go on like she has for so long. Something magical and life-changing would have to happen for this to work out.

The anxiety starts to build, as anxiety always does, growing multiple heads that threaten to devour her whole. *Meg will be married and have a life of her own…my mom will die someday…and I won't have anyone and I won't have money either…what if I get sick or have an accident or go insane…*

The phone rings, bringing Tania's anxiety attack to a temporary halt. It's Aditi. *She probably has more bad news*, Tania thinks as she answers the call. 'Hey,' she says feebly.

'You are not going to believe this!' Aditi yelps. 'Sit down. You are going to need to sit down.'

'Aditi, what is it?' Tania asks. She really doesn't need anyone adding to the drama in her head right now.

'Are you sitting down?'

'Dammit, Aditi! Just tell me already,' she says, grabbing a seat.

'Meera Anand wants us to do her sister's wedding!' Aditi sounds delighted about being the one to deliver the news. She loves being the bearer of dramatic news.

'Shut up!' Tania says in complete disbelief. She and Aditi had not even known that they were on the shortlist, and they had sort of written this wedding off. 'Please tell me you're not messing with me right now.'

'I'm not messing with you,' Aditi laughs.

'Because I've had the worst morning and if this is true...'

'It's true! We're signing the contract today!' Aditi says gleefully.

'Oh my god!' Tania lets it sink in. This is the life-changing miracle she needs. Once word gets out that they're doing Meera Anand's sister's wedding, every celeb and faux celeb in town is going to want to get in line. They just might have entered the big league. And the timing of it! Grateful tears roll down her cheeks as she tells Aditi she'll see her soon and rings off. It feels like the universe has gone out of the way to assure her that she is right to have faith against all odds. 'Thank you,' she whispers softly to an empty room.

5

'True love is hard work, not some magical ending. It's the reward reserved for those who don't give up after a substandard date or after discovering that the only good single men left in their city are all named Venkatesh.' – Meg

Meg is in the office ladies' room trying to make up her mind about whether she really wants to go on her very first set up date tonight – the set-up that she went to such annoying lengths to... well, set up. But that's the thing. Meg is highly introverted and prefers her own company at the best of times, and some level of regular interaction with the people she considers close. That's why parties and baby showers are not her thing. It's not that she cannot make small talk, it's just that it takes far more effort than she's willing to put in on any given day. Meeting new people takes a toll on her mentally and emotionally, and you can imagine what going on a date might do to her. *Do I want this badly enough to put myself through the ordeal of getting to know a random person over dinner,* she asks herself while putting on her eyeliner.

Plus, there's the embarrassing matter of never having been on a *date*-date. Relationships have always *happened* to her – organically evolving from friendships – and so this is all new. She has no idea what the rules are. There are always rules to this sort of thing, and Meg is the kind of person who needs to know the rules. She takes a breath. *I may not want this badly enough, but I want to prove my theory right so going on the date it is*, she tells herself. After all, how bad can it be? He's going to be really boring or the chemistry is going to be completely off or he's going to have one or two of the 116 mannerisms that completely turn her off. She'll survive. Besides, that's the worst-case scenario. He had come highly recommended by Suchi, who he was apparently very close friends with. And Suchi may be a lot of things, but she wasn't going to call a guy a 'real catch' unless he was one.

He's a dentist though. Meg is not sure how she feels about coming home to a man who has spent all day digging through other people's teeth. *At least he's always going to have work*, she thinks. Unlike Neel who had no qualms about quitting his job and moving back into his parents' house while 'figuring out' his career in music. The thought of Neel causes a vague concoction of emotions to rise up in her chest, and Meg shoves it all the way back down into the depths of her psyche – like she has been doing since she broke up with him. Feelings. They're like weeds in your otherwise thoughtfully nurtured terrace garden. They must be dealt with harshly or they'll destroy everything you've worked so hard to accomplish.

Tarsh, the dentist, has made reservations at The Grill, a somewhat fancy pub with excellent food. Perfect. Meg is hungry and the food is going to be exactly what she turns to for consolation if this date goes wrong. But so far, Tarsh is winning. For starters, his name is Tarsh (modern/generic, monosyllabic) and not say, Venkatesh (reeks of Chennai, trisyllabic!). It is scary how many people are named Venkatesh. Imagine meeting a really great guy, only to be told that his name is Venkatesh and having to make peace with that! *So this is why people call me an Anglophile.* She makes a mental note and shrugs it off just as quickly.

Tarsh also seems to have good taste going by the place he's picked (always a bonus). Meg checks her watch. It's only 7.35 p.m. Another 20 minutes to go. Perhaps she should order herself a drink while she waits. It might help her relax. It's not funny how often she's been told that she comes across as a finicky, uptight bitch the first time someone meets her. Or any time they meet her.

Meg is halfway through her drink and looking through the menu when Tarsh comes over to her. 'Hi, you must be Meg.'

Meg raises her head slowly to find the most good-looking dentist she's ever set eyes on in real life. She gulps. She wasn't expecting this. Sure, she had expected *something*, but good looks have never been her thing. It's just somehow never happened. She's never been attracted to anyone who was particularly good looking. Meg vows in her heart to break this toxic pattern in her life as she takes his hand. 'Tarsh, hi,' she smiles. 'Sorry, I started without you like the rude, socially-challenged person I am,' she mumbles.

'Not at all,' he assures her and orders his drink. He turns back to her very quickly like he can't wait to get to know this charming little person in front of him.

'So, how do you and Suchi know each other?' And that's just the beginning of the next two hours of a one-way conversation with, let's just say, a very heavy Suchi theme. Meg tries changing the topic, asks him about his interests.

'I like hiking,' he says and for a second, she's encouraged. 'I remember this time Suchi and I went on this amazing trek in...'

Ohh-kay then. She takes a ladies' room break to groan and texts Tania an update.

Meg: This is basically the Indian version of that romcom cliché where the two best friends are in love with each other but don't know it. Except in this Indian version, the woman is married.

Tania texts back in 10 seconds like a girl who's been waiting for live updates on her friend's date.

Tania: What? He's into Suchi?
Meg: Yup. So much for my plan.
Tania: Aw! Just get home, I'll cook anything you want for dinner. XOXOXO!
Meg: You are the best, Tania Rebello, but I fully intend to eat everything on the menu since he has already insisted that this is on him.
Tania: :D :D :D

~

'*Eppadi pochu?*' Muthu the watchman wants to know how Meg's date went. By now, everyone in the building knows about the bet, and Muthu seems to be the only one rooting for Meg.

'How do you even know...never mind!' Meg marches off into the lobby and takes out her frustration on the elevator button.

'Aiyo...*naat gooda?*' Muthu observes.

I tried, Meg tells herself as she gets into her pyjamas. But it's going to take her a while to mentally recover from this one. Two hours of Suchi-talk has completely drained her batteries. To think she made all that effort! Still, she can't help but feel good about the fact that she fought every urge to stay in her comfort zone, and did something that would normally be terrifying to her, all for the sake of the Goal.

Meg sits at her desk, pondering whether to write this in her journal or not. She decides this must be documented. She turns on her laptop and it flickers, goes out and has to be restarted. She restarts it and every app opens up on the desktop for her to shut down one by one. Among them is her super-secret writing app that she has been using to write a crime novel over the last three years. No one knows about it, not even Tania. Of course, it will never see the light of day because a) she'll never take it seriously enough to finish it and b) writing novels is for dreamers – those artistic types – and let the record reflect: Meghana Rao is not a dreamer.

6

'Sometimes, the universe throws a curveball your way just to see how you handle it. Do your best, surrender the rest and you'll pass the test.' #CornyThingsTaniaSays

It's been a week since they signed on Meera Anand, and Tania gets to meet her in a few hours. Like a young child on Christmas morning, our heroine spent all night tossing and turning, willing morning to arrive. Today is a milestone day for Ever After. Today, Meera Anand's name will be the glittery new addition to their client list. Tania paces back and forth as a thousand different anxieties demand her attention all at once: *Should I have made reservations at a fancy hotel? Will Meera like this place? Yay, we are officially glamorous. Am I wearing the right outfit? Will Meera approve? What if she changes her mind seeing that since I can't even handle my own looks, I can't be trusted with a big fat celeb wedding?*

After 20 minutes of pacing back and forth in their modestly-sized office space which used to be a crèche that Aditi's mother once ran in Adyar, she takes deep breaths, sits down and pours herself a glass of water. *Everything's going to be fine,* she tells herself. Even the stars seemed to be aligned. Susan Miller, the freakishly accurate astrologer did say that this is going to be her breakout year and that's that. No one's going to take that away from her.

After all, Meera approached them. And not because they have a ton of mutual friends. In fact, Meera's world is so far removed from her own that even friends of her friends aren't likely to come up on Tania's friend suggestions' lists on social media anytime soon. Which is why this victory is especially sweet.

'I loved your pitch instantly and that's that.' Meera's words ring in her ears as if she had said it to her. See, Tania hasn't even spoken to the dancer yet. Aditi usually handles the business side of things. It's for the creative direction and client management parts that Tania comes in. And while that's always been her forté, a tightening in the pit of her stomach warns her that this time, she might be a touch out of her depth. But in what way, she cannot tell. It's not like she hasn't spent nights doing the research, speaking to vendors, caterers, musicians and other performing artists and consulting trusted friends in related industries on what it takes to throw a celebrity wedding. And yet, something is off.

It was right there in the astrology too – an outer planet opposing her natal Venus. This always signalled the unfolding of something sudden, potentially exciting and possibly turbulent. Except the outer planet in question was going to be clashing with her Venus – which rules love and weddings – and therefore, looks particularly ominous to our heroine whose two main interests this year revolve around her love life and her wedding planning business. Tania hugs herself to shake off the blues. *It's going to be fine*, she tells herself once again and decides to ignore every bad vibe in the air for a change.

~

Meera Anand is the most exquisite creature that Tania has ever laid eyes on. Tania can't stop staring at her from across the table through dilated pupils, like she's having some kind of supernatural visitation. Carefully underdressed in jeans and a white shirt, hair tied in a casual bun and with barely any make-up on, Meera appears even more exotic than she did on the cover of last month's *Femina* if that's possible. Aditi, the far less impressed one of the two, to whom this is nothing more than their big break, is telling Meera about the beach wedding they recently planned for a small celebrity, and hoping Tania would snap out of whatever trance she's in and contribute to the meeting.

'You don't have to convince me,' Meera says with the hint of a smile, focussing entirely on Aditi. 'I'm happy to go with you. I don't know...I just have a feeling about this,' she shrugs. Tania watches her lips move in slow motion like she's undergoing hypnotherapy.

'You heard that?' Aditi nudges Tania in an obvious effort to get her to participate. 'She has a feeling about us!'

'Heh...eh...hee...uhh...heh...' Tania is the queen of eloquence this morning. She wants to say something – *anything* – but can't seem to get a word out. Thankfully, Meera is used to people forgetting how words works in her presence and isn't forming any opinions on Tania's level of competence just yet.

'Alright, ladies, couple of things I must clarify at this point though,' Meera says and Tania leans forward like she's at a storytelling session. 'Number one: this is my baby sister's big day, and I want it to be perfect.' Aditi and Tania nod and smile in understanding. 'Now, I know you probably hear this all the time, but if you fuck up my sister's wedding, I will make it my life's mission to destroy your careers, your reputations and ensure you never work again. Not in weddings, not anywhere.' She says this ever so calmly with the same hint of a smile she had at the very beginning of the meeting, making the totally unwarranted threat seem twice as disconcerting.

Tania is definitely out of her trance now and exercising every ounce of self-restraint to process what she's just heard without reaching out and clawing the woman's eyes out. Where did that come from? And how dare she? Aditi, on the other hand, seems to be matching Meera's inner poise. If this comes as a shock to her, you definitely can't tell by the placid smile on her unusually angular face, giving her a much-needed rough edge for situations like this. Aditi, unlike Tania, is driven by goals, not passion. And right now, she needs to get this wedding done, even if it means working under the direct supervision of Cruella de Vil.

'Do you understand?' Meera says.

'Absolutely,' Aditi smiles, her right hand instinctively reaching for the fist Tania has made under the table.

'Great. As you probably know, I shuttle between Chennai and Mumbai but I'll stay put in Chennai for the time being so we can work closely together.'

At this point, even Aditi can't fake her disappointment. 'Oh, but that's not necessary, Meera. You're a busy woman. And while I understand you want things done a certain way, why not let us work with your manager or someone? Someone you trust?'

Tania grits her teeth, takes Maria von Trapp's advice and tries very hard to remember a few of her favourite things (that iPad and so much more she could buy without a second thought just by having this client on board) so that she doesn't accidentally turn the table over and break Meera's jaw in the process. She wishes Aditi would be less nice about this.

Meanwhile, Meera looks at Aditi like she's about to *powerwomansplain* the hell out of her. 'I didn't get to where I am by trusting people with my hopes and dreams. So maybe you should save the cute suggestions and get to work already? We are going to be seeing a lot of each other, ladies.' Tania and Aditi can almost see the invisible fur coat made of skinned puppies around her shoulders as she rises from her seat and makes her way out.

~

Tania has an anxiety attack the minute she is on her way home and speed dials her mom, her calmer. 'I can't think of one good reason Aditi would want to work with her!' she says after bringing her up to speed.

'Oh, baby,' Tania's mother sounds like twice the mother hen Tania is. 'You don't have to do anything that makes you this unhappy, I hope you know that.'

Tania feels soothed already. That's really all she needs to hear when she's having one of her anxiety episodes: an acknowledgement of her feelings and the assurance that she will be loved no matter what she decides to do. Then she can go back to making the mature decision. It's really very simple, but most people don't get it. Meg definitely does not get it. How Tania wishes her mother were in Chennai too. But she's too attached to her house overlooking the hills in Kodaikanal, her life as a music teacher and her endless string of church activities. And this way, Tania gets to visit the hills often and it kind of evens out.

Tania lets out a long, happy sigh. 'Thank you,' she says. 'I'm so glad Meg is not the only person in my life!'

Her mom laughs and demands an update on Meg. Tania fills her in on the bet, but her mom can't seem to get past the fact that Meg and Neel are no longer together. Most people can't. 'Meg broke up with Neel?'

'Yes, Mom. Now focus on *your* daughter's non-existent love life, please.'

'But they made such a nice couple!'

'I know. But Meg has decided to move on and that's that. In fact, her mother is busy finding good Reddy boys for her. Oh, I'm sorry. Not Reddy. She corrected me the last time. But it makes me wonder...why aren't you doing the same?'

'You want me to find you a good Reddy boy?'

'No...'

'I don't know anyone in our family who's had an arranged marriage. It's just not a very Goan thing, you know? So I don't know how to help you there.'

'No, but I want you – as someone who knows what a relationship with a soulmate is like – to tell me what I can do to get myself one!'

Her mom laughs. 'It doesn't work like that, baby, and you know it. Besides, while I'd never trade the amazing years I had with your father, I also know what it's like to have it taken away. I'm not sure I'd wish that for anyone. I'm not saying all deep relationships end in the early death of one of the partners, but I know too many others like me who, having found that great love, had to let go of it at some point.'

'Great. Thanks for the pep talk, Mom. Now I'm motivated to find myself a mediocre love.'

'I support this plan.'

By the end of the call, Tania is back to her positive self again and determined to buy her very own villain suit and take on Cruella de Vil for the sake of Aditi, Ever After and that iPad she badly needs.

7

'There are no signs. Only coincidences. And good, old-fashioned common sense.' – Meg

Meg and Tania are out at lunch at The English Tearoom celebrating Tania's recent victory, Meera Anand.

'Well, she's hardly a victory,' Tania says, scanning the elaborate menu. Unlike Meg, Tania can't make up her mind when presented with too many choices. It's especially frustrating when she's really hungry and is also dealing with a personal crisis, causing all emotions to blur into one black hole of relentless emo-ness. 'That's it,' she slams the menu shut. 'You pick something for me.'

'Don't look so glum,' Meg says. 'I'm sure Meera Anand isn't as bad as you've made her out to be in your head.' Tania has a rich imaginary world, and this wouldn't be the first time she's seeing an otherwise ordinary – if difficult – person as some sort of mythical monster.

'You haven't met her!' Tania says. 'Ask Aditi, since you think she's the level-headed one.'

'Okay, this is supposed to be a celebration of your freedom from money issues, and I cannot believe I'm about to say this but...think happy thoughts!'

'You're right,' Tania says. 'Let's talk about something else.'

Meg nods in approval.

'Whose calls have you been dodging all morning?' Tania is quite sure it's Neel. She's secretly hoping that this is just Season 4 of Meg and Neel, where they both decide it's not working and start seeing other people. The following two seasons will be of things going hilariously wrong with their efforts to stay away from each other, until they realize in the season finale that they belong together. Silly Meg doesn't realize what she's got. How Tania wishes she had her own Neel. Someone who just feels right for her, whether or not he meets the ridiculous requirements of her list. Not that Tania even has a list.

'My mom,' Meg says and Tania is disappointed. 'She's been really sweet, calling and checking in on me, asking me to come and stay over. The other day, she even suggested we go watch a movie together!' Meg looks like she's coming down with a stomach infection.

'Why do you look so revolted at the thought?' Tania says.

'Because it's really weird! I mean, I know she's pleased with the fact that I've agreed to meet a guy she picks – thanks to you – but it's a bit much. Sweetness does not become her.'

'I get the weirdness of it all, but you should give her a chance. Who knows, maybe you might even like the idea of someone coddling you and find your own inner mother by extension.'

'Now, why does everyone keep telling me that? Like I'm not feminine enough or something. It's really annoy–' The phone rings, interrupting her rant. It's work.

'What is it?' Meg barks into the phone. 'No. I don't care what current trends suggest, but GIFicle is not a word and I will not allow it to be a thing under my watch. Your aim as a writer should be to write 500 real words that are so kick-ass that people don't mind spending the extra two minutes on our site. Got it?' She ends the call and sighs heavily. 'I have no hope for this generation… sorry, what were we talking about?'

'Finding your inner nurturing mother,' Tania grins.

'Shut up,' Meg says. 'So, I take it that you're still doing nothing about our bet?'

'Oh, I'm doing lots. Just not using conventional methods.'

'Conventional methods she says,' Meg sniggers. 'Like drawing energy from the new moon is any method at all.'

'You want to tell me again how your last date went?'

'Whatever. My point is, I *tried*. I put myself out there.'

'Along with your dignity and self-respect but please, go on.'

They bicker over the next hour and do no justice at all – being such picky eaters – to the exquisite meal.

~

'This is really about Neel, isn't it?' Meg finally asks on their drive back. 'It's more about me "belonging with Neel" than your interest in beating me at this bet.'

'I do think you belong with Neel, but I am also very interested in beating you,' Tania smiles.

'You know, I don't get that. I find it hard enough to get this invested in my own life. I just don't get so many people being upset by my break up with Neel... the neighbours, the watchman, my mom – *your* mom! It's crazy but it's almost like they see themselves in my story.'

'Oh…my…god…' Tania says, looking out the window as Meg pulls into the petrol pump. It's Neel. He's right there, paying the guy, but hasn't seen them.

'What is it,' Meg says, worried she's accidentally knocked off a cyclist – one of her perennial fears driving in Chennai, and follows Tania's gaze and finds herself freezing at the sight of Neel because a) this is the first time she's seeing him after the breakup, b) he looks unshaven and unhappy, the stubble isn't working for him and c) the coincidence of it all has her more spooked than she'd like to admit.

Neel gets into the car – his friend's car again, Meg observes disapprovingly – and drives away, but Meg can't seem to shake off the way she's feeling. It's the same feeling that she'd had in the ladies' room in the office before that date. Meg can't tell exactly what it is, but she knows that it makes her very uncomfortable.

'You know, Carl Jung used the term "synchronicity" to describe events that were not connected by cause and effect but by *meaning*.'

'Oh, just shut up already.'

But the meeting has made enough of an impact for Meg to mention it in her journal:

Ran into Neel. Felt strange, almost like it was prearranged. But it clearly wasn't and was just a random coincidence. Because logic.

Anyway. He's still borrowing cars from friends and walking around with that unshaven the-world-has-injured-me look so at least I know I was right to end things.

8

'Signs are everywhere. If you paid more attention to your third eye instead of shelling out cash on getting the perfect smoky eye, you just might finally see them.' – Tania

'Wake up!' a voice whispers in Tania's ear, and she promptly wakes up. It's 5.07 a.m. Three hours too soon for her to rise and shine. She could've sworn she really had heard a voice though. In fact, she can still hear it in her head. But it's just one of those dreams where you hear your phone or the doorbell ring as clearly as you would in waking reality. Except Tania can't brush this away as just a dream. To her, this is a premonition. The universe is trying to tell her something. Maybe it's a warning. Maybe she should be on high alert. But it doesn't feel that way. Deep in her soul, she feels the first rumblings of exciting news coming her way. She lazes in bed for a while pondering this. And before she knows it, the sun is about to rise. *It would be so nice to watch the sun rise for a change*, she thinks to herself and within seconds, she jumps out of bed and gets ready to go jogging. She's not a morning person but loves the idea of sunrises and morning jogs. And now that she's already up, it just makes sense.

She checks the time. It's 5.30 a.m. Perfect. It isn't that dark that she would need to carry her pepper spray, but it isn't full daylight either, so she still feels superior like morning people often do. She's definitely carrying her phone, even though there are no pockets in this particular pair of tracks, because there's no way she's missing out on an early-morning-sun Instagram post that will announce her new, morning-person avatar to the world. She plugs in her earphones, plays Tom Petty's 'Free Fallin'' and starts to run.

It's a lovely July morning. The road is empty, damp from the rain of the previous night, and the air, fresh and clean. It almost feels like it's wrong to be taking this in without paying some sort of subscription fee. Tania's heart is officially full. Not only with high-quality oxygen, but with hopes and dreams that only a morning like this can bring. She's going faster than her normal pace but doesn't feel it. The endorphins are doing their thing and inviting her into the happy place of her own mind. She takes their hand and lets them lead. They run through enchanted forests with flying horses that can transport you through time, space and alternate realities. Tania throws her arms around the magical, mind-reading flying horse and holds him tightly as he whisks her from one spectacular destination to the next. Tania, in her deepest heart, sighs and wishes she had that one special person to be alive with in this moment. The magical, mind-reading flying horse hears this, of course.

'Virus! Virus!' the unmistakable cry of a helpless man being walked – nay, dragged – by his untrained dog, snaps Tania out of the enchanted forest and back to early morning Chennai. She pulls her earphones out and turns around to find the world's worst-behaved golden retriever insisting on greeting her, while his clueless owner attempts to control him. The dog has circled himself around the man who is now skipping around the leash awkwardly, trying to untangle himself while ensuring his dog doesn't pounce on unsuspecting joggers. Tania, being the sucker that she is for gentlemen in distress, runs to his rescue, allowing Virus to lick her face to his heart's content.

'Great, you like dogs! What a relief. He's out of control!' the owner pants apologetically and the dog, sensing what is being said of him, makes a low growl of disapproval. 'Hear that?' he says. 'Golden retrievers are supposed to be the friendliest and easiest to train! I don't get it.' He appears to be in his mid-thirties – but you never know with beards, they're usually hiding a youthful but somewhat chubby face – and you can tell he's embarrassed about not being able to get his dog to listen to him.

'Wait, you named your dog Virus?' Tania is baffled by the idea of someone looking at an energetic furball of a puppy and saying, 'I think I'll call him Virus.'

'Yeah, I'm not very good with names,' he smiles awkwardly, instantly scoring points with Tania, who believes that men who are capable of blushing tend to be more self-aware and sensitive. 'I happened to be installing this anti-virus program at the time, and I was so frustrated at not being able to come up with a name for more than a week that I just gave up.'

Tania chuckles and goes to her knees to greet the unfortunately named Virus and bursts into fluent canine. Virus responds with furious wagging and face licking. He also, much to his owner's surprise, seems to listen to Tania. 'He's an angel, I don't know what you're on about!' Tania says between licks.

The man is not amused. Tania, though, thinks this is hilarious. Very Owen Wilson in *Marley & Me*, she thinks, making a mental note. He even has the charming dishevelled hair look to go with it. And the world's worst dog trainer? Not too shabby either. He's in khakis and a T-shirt and while his beard could use a trim right about now, there's something instantly likeable about his face.

Or maybe it's just the blushing. Yes, definitely cute, she decides. But before she can continue on that train of thought, Virus insists on tackling her to the ground, which she easily prevents by grabbing him firmly around the ears, looking him in the eye and saying things that only the two of them seem to understand. The owner watches on, completely impressed. '*Virus whisperer*. You're a Virus whisperer!'

Tania laughs. She gets up on her feet and dusts off her tracks. 'It's not magic, you know! Do you have a trainer?'

'No, but I'm definitely thinking of getting one. He's out of control!' he says again, and Virus growls.

'Tell you what,' Tania says. 'Ditch the trainer, I'll do it.'

'Seriously?'

'Yep. I'd love to get my own dog, but I can't really commit to it right now, so this is actually free therapy as far as I'm concerned!' She bends and scratches the dog behind his ears. 'Isn't that right, Virus? Isn't that right?'

Virus wags his tail merrily and makes approving noises.

'Wow...well...that's amazing...err...thank you!' The guy can't believe his luck this morning.

'You live around here?' Tania asks him.

'Uh, yeah. Two streets away! What about you?'

'5th Street. The building opposite Cupcake Station.' She bites her tongue as she says it. 'What's the need to blurt out your entire address to a complete stranger?' She can almost hear Meg scolding her.

Virus starts to get restless. He liked it better when the attention was on him.

'I'm Tania,' she stretches out her hand.

'Ryan,' He extends his hand, but Virus who is now beginning to sniff a juicy trail behind his owner, yanks him from behind, and he nearly loses balance. When he awkwardly regains it and tries to complete the handshake again, a car pulls up behind them and honks at the unfolding drama in the middle of the road, so Tania and Ryan say goodbye from across the road, and Tania promises to meet him at the same spot at 5.30 a.m. the next morning to begin obedience training.

Wow, the perks of being a morning person! Tania thinks to herself. She had forgotten the voice from her dream for a while, but now she has goosebumps thinking about it. The voice had woken her up. Now unless something even more unexpected was about to happen today, this must be it. What are the odds of someone who never gets out of bed before 8 a.m. going for a morning run, running into a cute-ish guy and committing to training his dog? Not that she thinks he's The One or anything. Our girl isn't *that* deluded. She only knows his first name. But this unusual event being preceded by such an uncanny dream gives her that sense that the universe is up to something good.

Tania is still in a daze as she reaches home and processes it all. *This was weird even for me*, she thinks as she reaches for her intention journal.

The number of things in my life that currently fit the symbolism of Uranus opposite Venus:

- *A big wedding planning opportunity, but the client turning out to be a bitch*
- *Meeting cute stranger on an unexpected morning jog, instantly falling in love with his dog and committing to train the dog which means I'll be seeing more of said cute stranger*

Not to get ahead of myself or anything, but what if this is the answer to my new moon intention? But then again, he's probably married, or not straight or something. That would be Venus–Uranus too. Sigh.

9

'Stick with the plan even when the go-with-the-flow types seem to be winning. It is so much easier to deal with disappointment when you know you've done EVERYTHING.' – Meg

'Meg, you're being stubborn and old school,' Nitin says after trying to explain to Meg for the last 20 minutes that blogs are dead, that brevity is everything and that GIFs instead of words work even better while attracting the young on social media. But Meg is not one to back down from an argument and especially not one that involves a topic so close to her heart.

'You say that like it's an insult,' she says, adjusting her perfect hair that needs no adjustment at all and proceeding to fold her arms across her chest.

'You know, I don't get it. How is it that someone who can't tolerate two extra syllables in her name is so anti-brevity?'

'Because a name that you have to say many times a day, depending on your relationship with the person, and useful information about a trend or product are two completely different things.'

'Fine, I'm done talking about this,' Nitin says, as he always does after an argument with Meg. 'But you'd better come with me to the meeting 'cause the client was very particular about being young and relevant.' It's been weeks since that rumour about the merger, and he's secretly pleased that the rumour turned out to be exactly that.

'The client is paying us to be good at what we do and to advise him on the best approach, not execute his every whim like a bunch of bots!' But Nitin has already walked away. So typical. Meg rolls her eyes and proceeds to lose herself in one of her recurring daydreams: she's running her own little agency, doing things her way and influencing trends, not succumbing to them. She's picky about her clients and only works with those who are capable of putting all their faith *and* money in her ideas. This make-believe agency is called Old School, of course.

'Crap!' Meg says as the reminder about their weekly conference call with STD pops up on her phone. In all her time at Red Dot, she has never forgotten the weekly meeting and is usually the one goading the team to get to the conference room 10 minutes early so they can all be prepared. 'I must really be preoccupied with the bet!' she says under her breath as she gathers her things and shouts to all the team heads to get to the conference room immediately.

'Your life as you know it at Red Dot is about to change,' STD's voice booms like the burning bush through the speaker phone in the conference room, making the hairs on the back of Meg's neck stand up. No, not because he sounds like Charlton Heston, but because of the recent rumours. But it's also just like STD to be dramatic. In fact, come to think of it, he's been using the 'Your life is about to change' line ever since she joined Red Dot. That's the other thing – STD lives in the US. No one, except the CEO who is rarely in, has met him. By all manner of appearance, Meg runs the place here. At one point, there was even a rumour going around that STD did not exist, and that Meg had made him up to keep everyone in suspended terror.

Not one person on the call seems to pay any attention to STD's big declaration except Nitin who looks at Meg nervously from across the table.

'I'm sure he's changed your designation again, Nitin,' Meg says to the head of client servicing turned head of creative production turned director of client engagement, pressing the mute button on the phone in an attempt to lighten his mood. By the way, those are all designations that STD has insisted on using at various points for the same person doing the *same job*. Everyone sniggers. They have all been through the revolving door of STD's 'We are a young agency, our designations need more fire!' mania at some point or the other.

'Or maybe he wants to quit digital and make bobbleheads again,' Satya, the production head contributes. Again, this was a serious conference call that happened six or seven years ago when STD tried sourcing bobblehead dolls in India for a client event and realized, to his shock and disappointment, that most people did not even know what they were. He, of course, decided that he would be the one to 'solve this problem' and drove Satya and Nitin nuts trying to work out a plan to start the first bobblehead doll store in the country. After two months of not doing the jobs they were all being paid to do, they'd finally got him to see the light.

'Or...or...' Neha, the social media manager chips in, 'this is about the public service campaign slash film slash flash mob slash stand-up act which we're really only making for people to notice us as a young, edgy and socially aware agency.'

There are snorts all around. 'Somebody please tell this man flash mobs stopped being cool about a decade ago. Wait, scratch that. They were never cool.'

'Hellοooo? Are you guys there?' STD is still talking!

'Uh, yes, Shawn, we're all here' Meg says, unmuting the call. Except no one has paid any attention to what he's been saying.

'So, what do you guys think? I just made the most important announcement in the history of Red Dot and no response!' Fuuuuuuck. Seven team heads on the call and not one person has heard the announcement.

'Hellοooo?'

Silence. As they all panic like school children trying to come up with a believable explanation. After a few seconds, Nitin cuts the call and texts STD saying the AC had leaked and that there had been water all over their desks and laptops, and he'd have to forgive them because they had all temporarily been focused on saving their laptops. As established, school children.

STD is not impressed. And he's not going to repeat all the exciting details for a group of buffoons who can't even handle a leaking air conditioner. 'The Warner & Parker merger is official. I know I've mentioned it before, but it's finally happening. Press release in a few days,' STD says when they're all back on the call. Nitin looks at Meg upset and betrayed like she had known all along and had kept him out of it. Meg tries to whisper across the table that she's just as horrified and that this is news to her as well. 'No reason to panic, there will be some reorganization and of course, you'll have to blend in with the new culture. But Hiten Shroff will be in town soon. He has extensive experience working in the US, and he's worked at Warner & Parker as well, so you guys are in good hands. I'm not sure, but I think he's joining in a couple of weeks. Meg will know what to do.'

How would Meg know what to do? Meg knows nothing about this Hiten Shroff except that he sounds like a relentless toothache. And the thought of adjusting to a new individual who just might have authority over her is upsetting enough to want to quit. Except STD has already seen this coming and will soon make her an offer she can't refuse: the Red Dot CEO in Chennai, Bijoy, will be fired and Meg will now officially oversee all Indian cities. All right, by all, he means two other cities. Meaning, more travel, more money, a greater sense of accomplishment and by extension, less sleep, less time for herself, less hope of winning the bet, which she had set as her major goal for the year. So, she hadn't gone to the extent of writing her intentions down like Tania, but she had said it out loud a couple of times. And when Meg declares her goals out loud like that, she likes to see them accomplished. Except this had once been a goal too. Hell, a dream, at one point. But now that she's actually here, she's decidedly un-psyched. Tania had said something on these lines the other day: 'Why does every emotionally fulfilling phase in my life have to be accompanied by an acute awareness of a different type of void?'

~

Meg drives back home with her head full of the events of the day: her mother's call this morning, asking if she has a preference for mustachioed men, and of course, Neel, who always lurks in the background like a clingy ghost. Suddenly, she feels like she's making no progress at all. The one thing she had – this job – suddenly looks more unstable than ever. And unlikely as it sounds, Tania's mysterious run-in with the golden retriever guy feels more like progress than her deliberate efforts. 'Okay, get a grip,' her inner tyrant-mother scolds her. *You're just spiralling...nothing has even happened. For all you know, the merger might be fun and you might find a great ally in this Hiten dude, and Neel...what do you expect? This is how a break up is supposed to feel. Be glad you're not falling apart singing sad country songs. And as for Mom, if you can ignore the moustache question, admit that you actually kind of like this closeness. Maybe not, but it's not so bad, Meg. It's just not so bad.*

'It's not so bad,' she says out loud.

10

'Be water, my friend,' – Bruce Lee. But also, Tania.

It's Obedience Training Day 1, and Tania can't believe how excited she is about rising early and training a stranger's dog. She parks herself on the floor and does her breathing exercises to centre herself. She does not know yet what the universe has planned for this mysterious encounter, and she must hold back from the temptation of assigning meaning to it – and have the patience to see how it unfolds naturally. After five minutes of observing her breath (it turns out that your centre is easy enough to find after all), getting into her tracks and calming Eddie down into a well-behaved ponytail with Moroccan oil, Tania is ready to start her session. She leaves the house and returns in a minute to grab the treats she had picked up for Virus the previous evening.

It's a misty morning as most mornings are at this time in any part of the world, but it's all new to Tania who seems to be seeing her world with fresh, morning-person eyes. *Wow*, she thinks to herself as she jogs her way into 10th Street where she was supposed to meet her student and his clueless owner. She's five minutes late, but there's still no sign of Ryan and Virus.

'Maybe they don't exist and my head just conjured them up to get me to become a morning person.' But immediately, the unmistakable sound of Virus barking in recognition from behind her convinces her this must be real. He's a couple of blocks away but loud as ever and running like a mad dog on steroids towards her, comically dragging his owner along with him. Tania holds on to the tree right next to her for support as the loving collision nearly knocks her down.

'I am so sorry!' Ryan is breathless. 'But he's all yours now.' He looks like he hasn't had any sleep and his beard could still use a trim, but Tania hasn't noticed any of this as she's too busy burying her face in Virus' super soft fur.

'It's all good,' Tania says with the perfect happiness of someone at the receiving end of canine love. 'We'll start working on him in just a minute – maybe two,' she smiles, looking up at Ryan for the first time today.

He, on the other hand, seems to have been watching her for a while. 'Such a dog person,' he says.

'Actually, I'm just an animal person,' Tania says. 'Grew up with dogs and cats and birds and squirrels, and I really miss that.' They start to walk but Virus isn't done with Tania. 'Come on, Virus. Let's go,' Tania says. Virus lies on his back in the middle of the road, demanding a belly rub. Tania wants to laugh, but as his trainer she cannot indulge him. 'No, Virus, not now,' she says in an authoritative voice. 'Walk! We walk now!' She tries to demonstrate by tugging gently at his leash. Virus, who thought Tania was a pal and not an alpha, does not like the authority she's trying to establish and lets out one of his low growls.

'Hey!' Ryan intervenes, but Tania gestures to him to leave it to her.

'That's not very nice,' she says in the human version of a low growl. Virus keeps staring at her, still lying on his back, trying to make up his mind about what he really thinks of her. 'Don't want to walk? Fine.' She drops his leash and starts to walk with Ryan, who seems a touch worried that Virus might run away. 'He won't run, just don't look at him,' she whispers to Ryan as they walk on. It takes a few seconds and Virus is walking by her side again and licking her fingers to announce his presence.

'Oh, look who's here!' Tania says. 'Will you be a good boy, Virus?' He jumps at her, searching her eyes to see if it's the same woman he met yesterday. She had been so much more fun even a while ago. What's got into her now? 'No, no, down.' Tania says. Virus makes a face that tugs at Tania's maternal instincts, but she knows enough about dogs to not give in. 'I said *down*,' she says firmly.

And to Ryan's shock and amazement, Virus obeys. He has tried this for the last three months, since he brought him home, to no avail. Well, he has to admit he lacks Tania's natural authority – and Virus has taken advantage of that to the point that the dog really thinks he's the boss.

'Good boy,' Tania says and Virus is back up with his forelegs on her torso. 'No,' Tania says. 'Down.' He's down again but looks hurt. Tania pats his head lightly and offers him a treat and he forgives her immediately.

'You got him treats?' Ryan asks.

'Of course. It's not fair to barge into a dog's life and expect obedience out of him without bringing him treats!'

Ryan smiles. 'Thank you. I really owe you.'

'Nah, like I said, this is free therapy for me,' Tania smiles back.

Virus yawns on cue to indicate that he couldn't care less whether the two humans are getting along.

After another half an hour of training, Tania manages to teach Virus three commands: 'down,' 'sit' and 'heel.' But the ratio of treat to obedience is embarrassingly disproportionate.

'I cannot thank you enough. Thanks so much for doing this,' Ryan says. 'Is there anything I can do...can I like...pay you or something?' He looks like he regrets saying it halfway through the sentence.

Tania makes a face. 'No, but thank you. I'm thoroughly enjoying this and it's filling a pet-shaped hole in my heart.'

'Okay,' Ryan says.

'You should get more sleep tonight,' Tania says as she walks away.

'How do you know I haven't slept?'

'It's all over your face!' Tania says. 'Which I noticed despite Virus.'

Ryan blushes and blurts out another awkward 'Thank you!' as she waves them goodbye. Virus acts up to indicate that he does not approve of Tania leaving. 'It's okay, buddy. You'll see her again tomorrow,' Ryan says, fully empathizing and kicking himself in his head for the thank you. Who says 'thank you' when an attractive woman declares that she has looked at him closely enough to notice he hasn't had much sleep!

Meanwhile at the apartment, Meg has had a Neel relapse. She's barely slept all night thinking about him and replaying their last conversation.

'I get what you're saying, but I just need some time, Meg,' he had said. 'You know that the band is at the verge of a breakthrough...'

'Yes, and I don't mean to sound discouraging *at all*, but you guys have been at the verge for a very long time, Neel. And while that may be the norm for a musician, I can't live like this. I don't want to waste your time either. This is a decision I'm making for myself.'

'All right. Name a few problems that you have with the

relationship itself...everything you're calling a problem is circumstantial. It has nothing to do with us. We're actually happy!'

'It's circumstantial because you refuse to make a decision... or a commitment for that matter!'

She can't recall the rest. By then they had started yelling at each other, and at some point during all the yelling, they had forgotten that they cared deeply about the other's feelings. And that was that. Neel had tried to talk to her later, but she had brushed him off saying it would be a bad idea. Of course, she has kept all of this from Tania since any suggestion of Neel having asked for time or another chance would only make her obsess even more about how they were meant to be. But on this particular morning, Meg feels the need to let another person into her predicament just for some clarity. She wishes it were someone more rational than Tania, but she's literally the only friend in her life at this point. Meg sits, legs folded, on Tania's bed, waiting for her to return from her training date with Virus but she's restless. The sound of the door being unlocked makes her jump.

'Hey! How did it go with Golden Retriever Guy?' her attempt at being casual gives her away all the more.

'Okay...' Tania eyes Meg suspiciously. 'Why are you in my room? What's wrong?'

'Oh, nothing. Just felt like chatting is all.'

Tania rolls her eyes. 'Spill!'

Meg obeys.

'Unbelievable!' Tania says at the end of the story. 'How could you not tell me? I knew something was off about Neel accepting your decision without a fight, but you never let me talk about it...'

'Are you done? Can I tell you what's bothering me now?'

'Yes.'

'I'm wondering if I should call him. I don't want to. I mean, I know nothing's going to change and it's honestly not fair to him that I keep going back and forth, and it's not fair to me to keep waiting endlessly for him, but I can't get him out of my head. I'm exhausted from trying to get him out of my head.' Meg lets out a yelp of frustration.

'Aww,' Tania appears to be moved by this admission. 'You already have what you're looking for! You're like that romcom heroine who has to go on many bad dates before she realizes that everything she was looking for was right in front of her all along!'

'Uhh, no. What I'm looking for is a grown-ass man who does not live with his parents, can give himself a reality check about his music and get a real job. And romcom heroines are stupid so no, I will not be realizing that.'

Tania sighs. 'Then what's the big dilemma you wanted to discuss? You clearly seem to have made up your mind.'

'The dilemma is this: I realized after the date I went on that I don't have the energy for too many bad dates. Also, there is no guarantee that I won't be wasting my time if I keep looking...'

'What I've been saying all along...'

'Wait. Neel, on the other hand, is like a known devil. And while I am wasting time thinking about him, I am clearly still drawn to him emotionally. Even though I know that emotions don't mean a thing if they aren't backed by action. The question is, do I continue to look for the guy who fits my plan or stick with the one I've already invested four years in?'

Meg's ruthlessly pragmatic approach grates on Tania's romantic sensibilities but she knows the only way to make Meg see her point is by speaking her language. 'If it were someone more adventurous, I'd have suggested keeping their options open. But knowing you, I think it makes sense to build on the four years you've already put into this relationship. I mean, unless you feel up to right-swiping or going the arranged marriage route with your mom.'

'That's the other thing' Meg says. 'I'm actually in a good place with my mother, and I know that meeting anyone she sets me up with would forever ruin our chances of happiness. So that's not happening.'

'But if you told her that, you'd ruin it anyway,' Tania says.

'True, which is why I'm not going to tell her. I'm just going to reject every bio she forwards to me with some legit excuse. Those aren't difficult to find, by the way.'

Tania slowly breaks into a smile. 'So…does this mean you're going to call Neel?'

Meg sighs. 'Yeah. Yeah, it means I'm going to call Neel.'

Tania squeals in delight. 'True love wins!'

~

By the end of the day though, Meg is not that sure anymore. 'This is just fear talking,' her inner tyrant-mother says. 'You've committed to this new plan, and now you're just chickening out.'

'No, I'm being practical,' Meg argues.

'So, practically, tell me what you expect out of this?'

'The same relationship, really. I don't expect him to change.'

'And you're good with that?' The tyrant is not one to give up on an argument.

'No, I am not. But I don't want to get stuck in an endless loop of bad dates!'

'So, don't. Call your mother. She's surely not going to pick some guy in love with a married woman. Guys on her list *want* to marry. It's fairly straightforward. Should work for you.'

'But what if it doesn't work? My mother and I will be back to square one. I know it.'

'So what? What was your goal for this year, Meg? Working on your relationship with your mother or finding the right person for yourself?'

This is enough to convince Meg, and she calls her mom while she's still driving to tell her that she's ready.

It has been a milestone day, Meg writes in her journal. *Not in my quest for love as much as in my quest for the mother I never had. I wonder what a therapist would say about my decision to not call Neel and go the arranged marriage route instead. No, scratch that. I do not wonder. Therapists are for weaklings.*

11

'Phonetics matter. In the long run, they do. Imagine having to say a name that distresses you and makes your body release cortisol every time you say it (like Venkatesh, for me). And no matter how much you love the person, you are still undergoing what I call "background stress" and in a long-term relationship, that stuff is lethal.' - Meg

Meera Anand wants to change everything about her sister's wedding. Beginning with the groom. But since that part of the planning is out of her hands (not for lack of trying), she has decided to give Aditi and Tania the time of their lives by attempting to control everything else. The 'quietly elegant' theme has now gone out of the window and she'd like everything a lot more 'out there'.

'Such as?' Tania enquires warily. Nothing distresses her more as a wedding planner, and as someone with a sense of aesthetics, as the words 'out there'.

'I don't know,' Meera says. 'You're the wedding planner!'

'Yes, but...'

'Yes, so plan something!' The vein on Meera's forehead turns an angry purple. One more valid question might be all it takes to wake up the brood of vipers asleep under her salon-treated hair. 'Golden roses, unicorns, the works! I want the perfect fairy tale.'

'Golden roses…' Tania takes the suggestion in. 'You mean artificial ones?' she dares to ask.

Meera wills the purple vein to disappear and addresses Tania calmly. 'Sure. Why don't we also use animal entrails as streamers at my baby sister's wedding?'

Tania takes a second to figure out that this isn't a serious request. She's at that point in a client meeting when she's mentally prepared to politely nod at anything. Like the time a client thought it would be a great idea to have live crocodiles at a children's birthday party, 'because we take children to the crocodile park, so why not?'

'No, Meera, it's just that golden roses…' Aditi tries to step in and find a good way to explain that golden roses don't exist.

'I know! They don't exist. If they did, this would be an actual fairy tale and I wouldn't need you. Get regular roses and dip them in gold paint! And the same for the unicorn. Get white horses and stick a rod through their foreheads. I don't care. Make it happen!'

'Wow,' Tania says once Meera makes an exit. 'She's taking this whole Cruella de Vil thing to a whole other level. Stick a rod through their foreheads?'

Aditi is in deep thought, like she's at the cusp of a master plan. 'We can change the brief, you know.'

'Meaning?' Tania is afraid at the very thought of angering Meera's vein again.

'Meaning,' Aditi reclines on her chair and puts her feet up on her desk in true villainess style, 'she was all worked up when she came in here. This isn't what she wants. Meera Anand does not have tacky taste, have you not noticed? This is what she's doing to send someone a message. Most likely, the person she was on the phone with when she entered, yelling those expletives at – aka the groom.'

'What? Meera doesn't approve of the groom?' Tania considers this for a second and connects the dots. 'Mmm...I did think it was fishy that she picked us when she could have had any of the big names.'

'Oh, she hates his guts,' Aditi says.

'But?'

'But the bride is stubborn and Meera's raised her since their mother passed away and well, it's complicated.'

Tania's eyes widen with curiosity. 'Wow! She told you all this?'

'I did my homework,' Aditi says. 'Half this job is knowing what strings to pull, what buttons to push and, more importantly, where to find them.' She looks pleased with herself.

'So, what about the groom? Did you meet him? Is he a cab driver that her sister threatened to elope with? Why is she hiding him?' Tania is now very engrossed in the story.

'What do you have against cab drivers?'

'Nothing. It's just that they seem to consistently feature in Chennai-based elopements.'

'Haven't met him, but he used to work with my brother-in-law and I hear he's a really nice guy.'

'Maybe *that's* Meera's problem.'

'Maybe.'

'And when are we meeting the bride?' Tania wants to know. 'I think it would be a lot easier for me to visualize the whole golden roses and unicorn wedding if I have a mental picture of the bride.'

'Heh. Soon. Let's hope Bridezilla is less terrifying than Cruella.'

~

Meanwhile, at Red Dot Meg is in the unfortunate position of being in charge of morale, which is at an all-time low since the news of the merger. It turns out that even seemingly adventurous people tend to love the status quo much more than they'd like to admit. There are rumours flying around about layoffs and people wanting to quit in anticipation. 'Guys, you need to calm down,' Meg addresses her flock. 'We all do. This whole merger thing may not be so bad. And no, no one in my team is getting laid off as long as I am around, okay? So please, don't make any rash decisions based on random assumptions...'

They stare back at her listlessly, like a Dementor has sucked out their collective soul. 'And there's an upside to all this,' Meg says, making a desperate attempt to cheer them up, 'We won't have to explain what Red Dot means to another client ever again!' The truth is, no one in the history of Red Dot has known what the name meant. Meg had once asked STD about it and he had simply asked her to close her eyes and said, 'Focus, Meg. What do you see?'

'Nothing,' she had said.

He suggested she look harder. And this went on for as long as it took for her to say 'Okay, I see it.' She didn't have to be specific about what it was she had seen.

'There you go. That's it. It's a red dot, Meg. *That's* what it means.' This story had always made her team crack up since it turned out that everyone at Red Dot had a similar story from their interaction with STD. On this morning, however, they are decidedly not amused.

'Okay, humour me,' Meg says at last. 'Put on your happy faces.'

'It's just that this Hiten sounds like a douche,' Priyanka, Meg's favourite copywriter, says.

'Every Indian male name that starts with H sounds like a douche,' Meg says matter-of-factly. 'It's a phonetic issue.'

'Hey!' Harish, the client servicing guy protests.

This, however, gets them all debating the douchiness of Indian male names that start with H and distracts them for a while. 'Hitesh, Himesh, Hardik, Hrithik... Oh my god! It's true!' Priyanka says. 'Meg's theory is true!'

'My theories are always true,' Meg says. 'On a serious note, we know nothing about this Hiten guy. So, with everything else that's going on, can we all please postpone zombie mode for later? Like when he actually shows up here and proves my theory right?'

They're in a mildly better mood now, and Meg needs her caffeine fix. She cannot believe what the world has come to – where *she* is left in charge of morale.

12

'Who decides when you're ready to kiss someone or hold their hand? Who makes up these ridiculous rules? And what if I'm more of a face holder than hand holder. What then? Rules are for those who lack imagination.' – Tania

It's been eight weeks since that first encounter with Virus and Tania and Ryan are getting along. But while the entire morning-walker community of the neighbourhood is aware of these developments, our leading lady and man are in stubborn denial. Actually, let's not speak for the man. For now. We don't really know what's going on with him except that he seems to be rather fond of his new dog trainer, which you can clearly see through that general air of dignified reserve. But Tania must have blinders on because she has somehow not noticed that Ryan has been opening up to her all week about his life (unusual for him given that he's a private person).

The life he left behind in Pune, running the family restaurant, his complicated relationship with his family, and that he's at a crossroads now in so many ways. In fact, she's so oblivious thanks to that voice in her head that's constantly warning her not to jump off cliffs for true love, that Ryan has to actually spell it out. 'You do get that I'm trying to say that you're special, right?' It is not easy for Ryan to vocalize his feelings but somehow with Tania, it's been different.

This seems to shake our heroine awake as she turns around dramatically in slow motion to look deeply into his eyes and connect with his lost, confused soul. And since Tania habitually confuses pity with love, she cups his face in her hands in a fit of spontaneity though their relationship is nowhere near hand-holding, let alone the face-holding stage. This in turn confuses Ryan, who thinks this means he's supposed to reciprocate but since he isn't wired like men of his age who casually go around kissing women, he cups Tania's face in his hands too and for a minute that feels like an awkward eternity, the two of them just stand there, not knowing what to do next or how to make it stop. Thankfully, Virus decides to bark and snaps the two out of their weird fairy tale reverie.

'Oh I...uh...I...should go...sorry...good luck,' Ryan mumbles incoherently.

Tania responds with equal incoherence, 'Uh, yes, me too. Of course. Yes.'

'Good luck?' Meg's non-existent belly jiggles until it hurts from laughing at Tania's romantic rendezvous under the coconut tree for all the early risers in the neighbourhood to see.

'Are you done?' Tania is not amused. Especially now that Nandu and Meenakshi Aunty are in the know. (Muthu saw them and faithfully delivered the news, like the friendly neighbourhood carrier pigeon that he is.)

'No! I won't be done for another week!' Meg laughs harder.

'You do realize that this is a lot more progress than you have made so far,' Tania points out.

'True. In the contest to see who can embarrass themselves more for true love, you definitely win!'

At this point, Meg's annoying laughing fit has driven Tania into her room to meditate. *But what about the thunder and lightning*, Tania wonders. She could've sworn she felt electricity surge through her body even through that awkward face-holding. But did he feel it too? Clearly, he didn't or he wouldn't have said 'good luck' of all things! What is that supposed to mean? Was it a goodbye? Was he never going to see her again?

'Stop it, stop it, stop it!' Tania scolds herself. She's clearly spiralling. This is no big deal. Yes, it was awkward, but it was also amazing. Which reminds her of Uranus opposing her Venus. This is exactly how those Internet astrologers describe Venus–Uranus transits. Like electricity. Like love at first sight or something just as bizarre. Something sudden and unforeseen. 'But Uranus also always comes with sudden disruptions and turbulence!' Tania starts to panic and calms herself down again. There's really no point overthinking this. Everything that has happened so far has happened out of the blue and whatever Meg might say, this is definitely way more progress than she has made. So yes, Tania will just continue trusting the universe, thanks very much.

13

'Falling in love is overrated, not to mention clumsy. I don't like falling into things. I'm more of the cautiously-stepping-into-love sort. Just look at Exhibit A (Tania). Is this really worth all the anxiety and indigestion?' – Meg

It has been a week since Tania's face-holding episode with Ryan and she hasn't seen him since. And as much as she'd like to brush it off as nothing, it's driving her endlessly crazy thinking of all the possible reasons why he would avoid her. After all, he did hold her face right back. And what about all the heart-to-hearts over the previous two months? Was that all just a Uranus induced lightning bolt that disappears as swiftly as it strikes? This whole drama is doubly stressful because she doesn't have his number. It had struck her as just a bit odd that they hadn't exchanged numbers until then, but Ryan seemed like someone who scared easily, and she had decided it was a better idea to wait for him to ask. But of course, she's not telling Meg just how much this is affecting her. Just not yet. She calls it curiosity instead and is busy trying to stalk him online.

For all his seeming straightforwardness, there is an air of mystery around the guy. For starters, he seems very interested in her as a person (he told her she was special but he could have meant that as a friend) but hasn't particularly shown any romantic interest apart from the face-holding which could've just been… well, something else. This is odd for someone like Tania who is very accustomed to being hit on all the time. Also, there was no mention of friends or a girlfriend. And now, he seems to be completely absent online. She has tried every possible spelling of Ryan Mendonza but cannot find the guy. Unless you count that one profile with the Siddharth Malhotra display picture, in which case she'd have to reject him by default. And now Tania is worried that he may be carrying some huge secret.

'Like what?' Meg says. 'Ooh, maybe he's a vampire!'

'I'm serious,' Tania says. 'What kind of person leaves absolutely no trail on the Internet? Maybe that's not his real name.'

'And why would he do that? Why would any guy not reveal his real name to a woman as delightful and attractive as you? No, I'm serious.'

'It's happened before…' Tania raises an eyebrow. She means Kunal. The douche who juggled them both but to whose douchiness they owed their friendship. While Meg was the one who had been in a long-term relationship with Kunal, and was – in the real sense – the betrayed party, Tania had taken it much worse. It usually takes Tania about an hour to fall in love, and she had managed to love Kunal much more in six months than Meg could in four years. She remembers the whole scene like it was yesterday.

She had been exchanging steamy texts with him all afternoon and he had invited her to his place – which turned out to be the apartment he was sharing with Meg – in the evening. Meg had had a string of late nights at work and wasn't expected home until later but as these shady stories usually go, she had come in hours before she was expected and Kunal was still in the shower prepping for his mid-day booty call while his phone buzzed off the hook and Meg happened to see the incoming messages. To cut a long, embarrassingly clichéd story short, Tania had landed up immediately after and found out that the guy she had already planned a wedding with in her head was just another garden-variety creep.

But while Tania was devastated, Meg was furious. She had insisted on throwing Kunal out of the apartment, but it had turned out that the lease was in his name, and so she ended up without a boyfriend and an apartment literally overnight. It worked out serendipitously though because Tania had been on the lookout for a flatmate. For lack of any alternatives other than moving back in with her mother, Meg had said yes. She had planned to move out as soon as she found another place though because 'it's just too weird,' but the two had ended up bonding over their mutual misery and loathing of Kunal.

'Are you serious? Are you really still not over that dipshit?' Meg is shocked. It had taken her no time at all to move on from Kunal.

'What? Of course, I'm over him. But these things leave scars. And I have to be careful. What if this guy is hiding something, Meg?'

'Okay, first, you're being paranoid. Secondly, nothing romantic is going on between you two just yet. Face-holding notwithstanding. So technically, he's not *hiding* anything, even if he is. Thirdly, there's something very attractive about a person who doesn't feel the need to be on social media, and it's kind of absurd that you take that to mean he's hiding something.'

Tania takes a deep breath. 'You know what? You're right. I'm overthinking this. It's just that I've grown…fond of him.'

'Oh baby, you're completely smitten. And that's okay, you can admit it. There's no rulebook for how long it should take to fall for someone. Though if you ask me, I think a year is a reasonably good time frame.'

'Oh, why am I like this?' Tania sinks into the sofa and throws her legs over Meg's lap. 'But enough about me. I am dying to hear about the call with Neel. Didn't want to start that conversation till we had enough time…'

'Yeah, about that…'

'Don't tell me,' Tania says. 'You changed your mind.'

'There's more.'

'Oh god,' Tania winces. 'Please tell me you didn't call and make it worse and now you're never going to get back together – even in season 10?'

'No. I didn't call Neel.'

Tania lets out a sigh of relief.

'But I called my mom and told her I'm ready to meet any guy she wants me to meet.'

'No!'

'Yes.'

'But what about everything we discussed? What if it goes wrong? What if…'

'I don't care, Tan. I have to keep moving forward, and I have to take matters into my own hands or I won't be… me. I have set a goal for this year and it's simply not me to sit back and make excuses to go back to my old life. So there.'

'So there,' Tania says resignedly.

~

Tania's journal entry for the night:

Pulled the Knight of Cups from the Rider Waite deck for the question, 'What is the current situation?' Should've left it at that because the universe was basically telling me that love is coming my way. But then I had to ask the follow-up question: 'What is the big-picture meaning of this relationship?' Tower. I got the TOWER! I'm anxious now. I mean, sure, the Tower isn't all bad and really is about opening up to a higher level of consciousness but I'd be kidding myself if I let myself think it's coming without massive turbulence and destruction at some level. But serves me right for consulting the tarot and not being prepared to hear the truth. This Tower symbolism ties right in with Uranus. I'm not sure how to proceed or even if I'd be given much of a choice in this situation. God, I wish I knew more astrology than 'Uranus is opposing my Venus' right now.

14

'The problem with people who insist that you must always go out there and do something is that they have never paused to consider that this direction is kind of vague.' – Tania

Hiten Shroff has finally made an appearance at Red Dot and it turns out, that he is not a douche at all. In fact, he's very likeable. And kind of cool with his vision of making Red Dot W&P (which is the unfortunate name they'll be going with) the hipper, younger, digital cousin of the traditional advertising agency. If the memo from the corporate office is anything to go by, he's 'here to revolutionize'. He also happens to love the word 'revolutionize'. With the 'z'. Which is also the title of his upcoming book on digital trends. A digital guru *and* a celebrity. What's not to love? He's everybody's new blue-eyed boy – and Meg's worst nightmare.

For starters, he always says 'old school' like it's a bad word. And he's taking over the place with his ridiculous anti-gravity hairstyle, fake American accent and making everything 'hipper'. While he's looking forward to working closely with Meg whom he's heard so much about, our heroine is going to turn him into the douche she expected him to be by constantly undermining his authority because she strongly disagrees with his ideas.

The truth is, she's more afraid of losing her place as 'The One Who Holds It All Together' at the agency.

'Sooo, we're going to have to lose the long copy,' Hiten says at a meeting and almost on cue, everyone turns in Meg's direction.

'What?' Meg snaps. 'You heard him! Lose the long copy.'

'Uhh, is there a problem?' Hiten asks flashing a dimple tentatively. He has no idea how many of Meg's rules he's broken since his arrival and how much she fantasizes about brutally taking him down.

'The problem, Hiten, is that everything you've been suggesting since you got here is butchering the English language. And as the person who heads the copy team, I have to say no.' Meg tries her best to appear calm and self-possessed but it's becoming increasingly impossible with everyone clearly leaning towards the new guy. The tension in the air rises as everyone immediately senses a Meg-a-rant coming. Hiten is a touch thrown and you can tell. He's been playing nice until now because, well, that's his default persona. But if Meg wants a fight...who is he to disagree? 'But saving the English language is the role of the English teacher, not the digital agency that must stay on top of trends.' *Ooh*. Could he be the Anti-Meg that the seers and prophets long foretold? The copywriters start shifting in their seats, wrestling with their divided loyalties to Meg who has had their back for so long, and Hiten who is saying the very things they've been trying to get Meg to see for so long.

'But as the person responsible for the quality of writing that goes out of this agency, I think this is my call.' Meg is at that point where she knows she's on thin ice but can't help but stomp harder. She's not going to let some guy with a name starting with 'H' just walk into her house and tell her what to do.

Hiten, sensing the tension in the room and not wishing to undermine Meg any further in front of her team, decides to let it go. 'Meg, I think we should talk about this later.'

'Nope. Whatever you have to say to me, you can say in front of them,' Meg's self-destructive streak is clearly running the show now.

Hiten sighs and responds calmly. 'Well, then you should know that the final call is mine, especially as it relates to the new vision for the agency.'

Meg stops for a heartbeat, picks up her things, excuses herself and leaves the room. The minute she's in the ladies' room, though, she bawls like a toddler whose parents are presenting a united front against her. It's humiliating but, most of all, it's making her extremely insecure at a time when she really needs this job to be the most stable thing in her life. And all the mixed emotions blur into one black hole: Neel. She wants to see him. She *needs* to see him. He had this nearly magical ability to calm her down. 'Stopitstopitstopit!' she says under her breath. 'Don't go there. Just. Breathe.'

She breathes in and out until her heart rate slows down, but the Neel spiral is only getting worse. If not for her highly developed self-restraint, she'd be back with him by now. She must do something about this. This can't go on forever. She has to move forward but this irrational emotional vortex is sucking her in. But more importantly, she must do something about Hiten. Perhaps talking to STD might help. Or perhaps not. She has to be smart about this though. No more open confrontations. She must learn to be sly like him and beat him at his own game. Even if that means sucking up to him temporarily. It's going to be humiliating, and she's going to want to quit. But if she is to stay committed to her goal for the year, she must do everything in her power to stay afloat at work.

~

'You know, Aditi knows this really nice therapist who was a huge help to one of her friends who was unravelling after a divorce…' Tania says as Meg relates the events of her day later that evening.

'You think I'm unravelling?'

'No, but I know how much your work means to you – it's a big part of your identity, so it might help to talk this out with a professional. I mean, you just might learn how to deal with this guy so that things don't get worse. Especially not this year.'

'*Please*. Psychotherapy is a rip-off. Especially in this country. Did you know that they don't even have a couch? That's just wrong. The couch is central to therapy…'

Tania places a business card in the palm of Meg's hand and closes her fingers over it. 'Just in case,' she says and makes a quiet exit while Meg stands there staring at the card. 'Shyama Nambiar, Psychotherapist, Couple's Counselling' it reads. Meg rolls her eyes but puts the card in her wallet.

Just in case.

Meg makes her customary to-do list before getting into bed:

- *Return Mom's call*
- *Mess with Hiten by pretending to suck up to him*
- *Consider looking for another job? Gah – maybe not yet*
- DO NOT CALL THE THERAPIST!

15

'The universe doesn't give a crap about our deadlines.' – Tania

'That's it! I'm done with this!' Tania is at her wit's end with Meera Anand's tantrums. The whole point of not having a day job is that she could pick who she'd work for. And this is increasingly beginning to feel like a deal with the devil. This time, Meera has changed her mind about the caterers, the band and the wedding invitation designer she had originally approved of and confirmed. This puts Tania in the very awkward, and not to mention unprofessional, position of breaking the news to the respective parties. The designer had been so excited, she had even started working on the rough sketches. 'It just doesn't make sense anymore. I don't care who she is, but I'm done!'

Aditi listens quietly as Tania rants to her heart's content. Tania is usually the one talking Aditi through client drama, and this is a first. Meera has really pushed her around.

'There's something I've been meaning to tell you,' Aditi says once Tania calms down.

'Oh my god, I feel like you're about to give me an extremely good reason to not quit this thing.'

Aditi laughs half-heartedly. 'It's been bleak on the financial and emotional front lately...you know my mum-in-law is unwell, right?'

'Yeah,' Tania nods, concerned.

'The hospital bills have been piling up, and we've been managing but Rakesh got laid off last week and he's coming back to India. I'm not sure how long it will be before he finds a job and things stabilize again, but in the meanwhile there are school fees and more hospital bills and...just...life...' Aditi's voice breaks – Aditi is the kind of person whose voice *never* breaks.

'Hey!' Tania reaches out to pull Aditi into a hug. 'We'll figure it out, okay? It's just money. We'll figure it out. Forget about my Meera rant. I'll do anything to help you.'

Aditi smiles, her eyes welling up. 'I love you, Tania. Thank you,' she says and walks away to pull herself together.

But there's something else bothering Tania. It's been 11 days and Ryan and Virus still haven't shown up for their morning sessions, and since they don't have each other's phone numbers yet, she's just going to have to wait this out. Combined with the online invisibility cloak, Tania's got a queasy feeling in the stomach. 'Stop overthinking it!' she scolds herself. 'You've got bigger problems.' She sighs. Ryan is the only thing that was keeping her going through the Meera stress, and now it looks as though he might just be a whole new source of stress. And if this isn't the magical encounter arranged by the universe, then what is it? Surely there had to be a purpose, what with the totally unexpected way in which he appeared in her life. And that dream! But what if it's not what she thinks it is? What if he's not The One? The Tower card flashes before her eyes again, and Tania feels a churning in her stomach. What about her intention to meet her soulmate this year? Should she take a page out of

Meg's book and become proactive about it? Nothing too out of the way, maybe join a class or something? She should at least go to places where her chances of meeting someone are higher. At least that's what Susan Miller, the astrologer she's been reading, likes to say. That astrology only shows the timing of events and it's up to us to make the best of the opportune time.

'Shhhhhhh!' she hushes her mind and decides to consult the tarot. After the rituals are done, Tania sits on the floor, legs crossed and asks the question: 'What is your advice about Ryan? She begins shuffling and a card comes flying out. It's the Hanged Man. Tania *hates* the Hanged Man. It's a card with the image of a man hanging upside down. It usually pops up when one is about to have a massive change of perspective about something. Sometimes, it's about being in a state of limbo and waiting without knowing. She puts the card back inside and tells herself it doesn't count since she has to pull it out in order for it to qualify.

She starts to shuffle again and once again, the Hanged Man comes flying out. Tania feels a tug inside her chest. She knows this only happens when it's really *the* card. She sighs, picks up the card and looks at it like it's a person. 'Fine. Be like that.' She hates it when the cards insist on telling her something she doesn't want to hear. She decides to outsmart the cards by asking another question though she knows it's futile. 'Should I go out more? Socialize? Join a group or class maybe so I can find this person? Should I put myself out there or should I just...be?'

After a while of shuffling, she pulls a card. The Hermit. 'Very funny,' she says and with that, the cards are packed away and the closet door slammed shut.

But deep down, Tania feels validated for her intuitive sense to just go with the flow instead of trying too hard. 'It's going to be fine,' she tells herself before her thoughts spiral into the Ryan hole all over again.

The doorbell rings. It's Nandu. She's a small woman in her fifties with very short hair that looks like she cuts it herself. She's come bearing khichri and is still wearing her apron. It's just something she does – show up at people's doorsteps with food – when she's been left waiting too long for the gossip she so badly craves. Her only redeeming quality is that she likes to get said gossip from the horse's mouth. That way, it doesn't quite qualify as gossip and makes her appear vaguely affectionate.

'Oh, Nandu,' Tania can't hide the disappointment in her voice. She isn't expecting visitors and a part of her had hoped that Ryan would come looking for her. It couldn't be that difficult for him to find her house. All right, it would be excruciatingly difficult but that's what leading men are supposed to do.

'I am detecting a lot of heartache,' Nandu says, letting herself into the house. 'See? That's why I brought khichri. It's very good for heartache.'

'Did you mean heartburn maybe?'

'*Haan*, same only.'

Seeing that Nandu isn't about to leave anytime soon and with Meg away at work, Tania gives up, closes the door behind her, grabs her bowl of khichri and settles down on the futon.

'Now, come on, tell me everything,' Nandu says, her face beaming with the anticipation of the mega plot twists in her favourite soap. Also, she loves that she gets to be the one to give Meenakshi Aunty the news.

Tania groans and tells her sad tale through a mouthful of khichri. It's good – there's that at least.

'I am telling you,' Nandu says at the end, 'these modern boys are like this only. Holding your face and running off. Just say the word and we'll find a good Chennai boy for you.'

'Nandu, I'm the one who held his face first,' Tania says but Nandu will not hear of it. This isn't how she likes her soaps ('girls must never make the first move') and she prefers to remember it the way she likes it, thank you very much.

But after a whole hour of listening to Nandu give her really bad advice, Tania is determined to close the Ryan chapter and move on with her life. Sure, she's on a deadline to find love but this is clearly not working. After all, she has enough on her plate at work and she's just going to have to focus on that. She owes this to herself. And the khichri.

16

'Things fall apart. But that is exactly when the centre must keep holding on, Yeats.' – Meg

It is a Saturday afternoon in early October and Meg has 12 profiles of prospective grooms to sift through. This is her mother's shortlist. The longlist went up to 37. 'You can take your time but if you ask me, the US-based microbiologist seems perfect. But no pressure, no pressure!' her mother had called in early to give her a mini-migraine.

'Thanks, Mom. Now I'm going back to sleep,' Meg had lied before she hung up, jumped out of bed and opened her laptop. Hours later, she's still in her pyjamas researching one specific prospective groom on the Internet: Rajeev Menon. He's not the US-based microbiologist. He's a Bangalore-based architect running his own business and seemingly thriving, since he's currently on a business trip in Europe (as social media stalking showed her). There are pictures too. He's tall, has dark, inset eyes and not much of a jawline. Not devastatingly good-looking (which, for Meg, is a good thing), but attractive. There are many pictures of buildings, ruins and architectural marvels from across the world (but of course) and food (she can live with that), no selfies (hallelujah!) and pictures that have a recurring set of three or four friends (an introvert). So far, perfect. He seems self-contained and respectable and totally Meg's type. At least the type she's aiming for.

'But it just strikes me as somewhat dubious…that a man like this should go for an arranged marriage,' Meg thinks aloud later that evening as she holds his profile open for Tania, who is relaxing, sipping some hot chocolate.

'Uhh… because clearly there are women like you stalking him on the Internet and poring over his typo-free words?'

'It's true,' Meg smiles fondly. 'He's got good spelling. But that still doesn't answer my question…'

Tania rolls her eyes. 'You are so judgmental, you know that?'

'Huh?'

'Look at you judge a guy for choosing an arranged marriage when that's exactly what you're doing.'

'I wasn't judging, I was wondering about the loophole...'

'Well, what's the loophole with you?'

'There's no loophole. I just…don't trust my offline self to make prudent relationship decisions,' Meg says after some consideration.

'So, there you go. He probably has just as bizarre an excuse.'

Meg smiles hopefully as she zooms in on his picture. 'He could be *The One*, Tan.'

Tania snorts and spits hot chocolate all over Meg.

~

By Sunday, Tania is restless. She's the kind of girl who likes to go out on the weekends, but of late it seems like all of her friends have conspired to make some sort of pact to be reclusive, and leave her out of it. Preity is busy with the new baby, Suchi has been avoiding her ever since Meg's date with her 'best friend', and three others have left on a hiking trip that Tania couldn't be a part of thanks to Meera Anand's separation anxiety. Aditi has enough on her plate to be thinking of relaxation, and the rest are scattered across different parts of the world.

And there is always the matter of Ryan's mysterious disappearance. But then again, she hasn't gone for her morning walk the last couple of days either, and she wouldn't know if he had returned. From wherever. She jogs her memory to see if she might have given him an address at some point. She did tell him which building she lived in but that's not specific enough, and he'd have to be quite crazy to come looking for her. Which he clearly is not. Or is it really that crazy?

Stop it, she scolds herself. 'Just for once in my life, I want the guy to be fretting over me! I'm always the needy, anxious worrier in the relationship. I'm tired!' she tells Meg.

'So don't be clingy and anxious,' Meg is focused on the book she's reading across the living room but is also aware that Tania needs attention right now.

'I said needy, not clingy,' comes the angry retort.

'What's the difference?' Meg says, still reading.

'Uhh, clingy people make you responsible for their neediness by attaching themselves to your life and questioning your every move. Needy people just feel needy. They don't impose themselves on you in anyway and quietly suffer. How can you not know this?' Tania almost sounds offended.

'Right. So, don't quietly suffer. Don't suffer at all. Don't make someone so central to your existence.'

'Excellent advice. You have such a gift for counselling,' Tania says.

Meg finally closes her book and sits up on the couch. 'For the record, I've been missing Neel like hell since we broke up. But I've resolved to not let those feelings sabotage my future. I want to move forward so I'm doing that. Mind over emo fluctuations is my policy – and it works.'

Tania sighs heavily. 'You're either extremely healthy or damaged beyond all hope.'

'Maybe, but at least I'm spending my weekend reading a book, connecting with an architect and coming up with a diabolical plan to take down Hiten Shroff while you are making yourself sick with worry over a guy with whom you have nothing concrete going.'

This feels like a slap in the face. 'You know what, you're right.' Tania rises from the living room floor with a new resolve. 'Enough about this guy. Enough resolving to not think about this guy. Or any guy. I'm going out.'

'Where to?'

'I don't know, somewhere fun and weekendy.'

'Who with?'

'Just me and my higher self.'

'Oh, but I can't make it.'

'Not you, my… very funny!' Tania swishes her hair like a diva and charges into her room to get dressed. 'No getting hung up on anything or anyone specific. Ask for what you want and raise your vibration to its frequency,' she tells herself and appears pleased like someone who has received the best advice.

17

'I'm not into heart flutters. I'm into solid commitments bound by a contract.' – Meg

It's Monday and everyone at Red Dot is a touch concerned about Meg who entered the office whistling 'Happy' today. She's been noticeably happy too, getting along with Hiten and making it look genuine.

'Okay, I'm not buying it. What's really going on?' Nitin enquires during lunch.

'What do you mean?' Meg asks. She's been so spaced out all day exchanging DMs with Rajeev Menon that she hasn't realized how odd this must be for people who've known her forever.

'I mean, what's with the whistling and the laughing and the getting along with Hiten thing? Genuine or diabolical plan?'

'Oh, I actually haven't thought of Hiten all weekend. Can you believe it?' This is a lie, of course, but it almost seems that way since the email and text exchanges with Rajeev started. Besides, Meg is feeling let down by her colleagues and team for being so easily swayed by Hiten's attempts at 'revolutionizing' the place and isn't about to let them into her diabolical master plan.

'I can't, actually,' Nitin says. 'Hey… how are you?' This is the first time he's asked since the argument with Hiten went badly.

'Peachy!' Meg says defensively but looks like she means it even though she's yawning incessantly. Nitin is confused but decides to leave it alone for the time being. Maybe she's having a nervous breakdown, who knows? He'd just have to deal with it later.

Meg is too distracted by her phone to notice Nitin's bafflement about her sudden cheerfulness. She and Rajeev have been at it since about 9 p.m. the previous night. She's barely slept but it's been so worth it. She hadn't counted on someone her mother picked out to be so fun. Rajeev seems perfect. He reads, but mostly architecture-related books, is in his own words: 'introverted to the point of manic reclusion at times', enjoys movies and Netflix when he wants to unwind, which is rare, absolutely loves his job, gets to travel and is an unapologetic foodie. *And* he moved out of his parents' place immediately after graduation because he couldn't imagine becoming 'one of those guys'. He's the Anti-Neel. But more importantly, he's the male version of Meg. They are both currently at that stage where they can't believe such a person even exists, let alone that they've had the good fortune to cross paths. Were they any less rational, they might have even used words like 'magical'.

Meg's phone beeps. It's Rajeev again:

`Have a couple of minutes between meetings and I'm using it to say hi to you instead of grabbing a coffee.`

Meg's heart flutters but she hushes it down. She is not a fan of heart fluttering. Nothing good ever comes of those.

Meg: `And he calls himself unromantic?`

Rajeev: `Flowers, holidays, cooked dinners and surprise birthdays are romantic, I've been told. Texts definitely don't qualify.`

Meg: `Who made that list? Someone from the fifties?`

Rajeev: `I cannot believe how alike we are…or seem…and that's my two minutes. Talk soon.`

Meg smiles, holding the phone to her chest in the empty room. Heart flutters aside, she does not approve of developing feelings for people she's known for a few hours. But this isn't about feelings yet. This is about a ridiculous level of compatibility. If she didn't know her mom as well as she does, she might have even suspected a practical joke. And for the first time in a while, Meg feels like she's making progress on her year's big goal. And that alone makes everything else – even the Neel pining and Hiten douchiness – bearable.

'It's not about flutters,' she tells herself. 'It's about the Goal.'

~

Tania is on the fence about Rajeev. On the one hand, she's happy for Meg. But something about this isn't quite right. Is someone exactly like oneself the best we can do? Where are the lessons there? Where's the balance? And god knows, someone as one-sided as Meg needs a counterpart. And as much as she hates being that friend who can't let go of the idea of her friend with someone specific, Neel was that counterpart. It was perfect! He balanced her out and you can actually have this verified – Meg was so much more likeable when he was in her life. He drew her out of herself, made her easy going around company, brought her to life! But Tania is nothing if not fair. She doesn't know this Rajeev guy. Hell, Meg doesn't know him. What if he is nice too? Besides, no one understands the mysterious ways of the universe.

'Sooo...have you told your mom yet?' Tania enquires after a while of watching Meg stare at her phone with a big grin on her face.

'Uh...what?' Meg says after a few distracted seconds.

'Have you given your mother the good news?'

'What news? There's no news.'

'Are you serious? I am watching your teen drama live! How can you not tell her considering you met him through her?'

'Okay, first of all, she doesn't know him. His was one of her shortlisted profiles and yes, I'm very grateful, but I'm not going to tell her anything until I'm sure it's going somewhere.'

Tania is completely baffled. 'So you're only going to tell her when you get engaged to him?'

'No, I'll tell her when I'm about to meet him.'

'Which is when?'

'I don't know, it hasn't come up yet. He's going to be in Singapore for a while – it's not easy.'

'Oh, please!' Tania snorts.

'What?'

'It's just you two over-cautious freaks being hell bent on taking it slow like there's some rule book!'

Meg pauses and turns to look at Tania for the first time through the conversation. It's true. Rajeev and she have been chatting nonstop and they've talked about everything from childhood trauma to pet peeves to current work stress, but they have somehow circled around, without touching, the big question about the next logical step: when should we meet?

'You're right,' Meg says at last. 'I'm going to ask him to meet me.'

'Good,' Tania says. 'But maybe you should tell your mom first.'

Meg groans but agrees and calls her mother to give her the

glad tidings: that she had been right all along about how well she knew her daughter. 'Do I have to?' Meg makes one final plea.

'Yes!' Tania has her stern face on and Meg obeys.

Once Tania leaves the room, Meg reaches for her Filofax and makes her to-do list:

- *RAJEEV*
- *RAJEEV*
- *RAJEEV*
- *RAJEEV*
- *RAJEEV*

18

'If you love something, set it free and proceed to exhaust yourself by obsessing about its whereabouts because when it finally returns (and it always does when it's real), there is nothing quite like that feeling.' – Tania

It's been 22 days, seven hours and 23 minutes since Tania last saw Ryan. Not that she's keeping count or anything, but she's been anxious. Not only because this might mean he's a dodgy guy but because something horrible could've happened to him and Tania does not like that thought. This has always been a problem in her relationships when the guy went MIA for a while. She'd start to get mad and feel really sorry for herself, but then an anxiety attack would take over and make her feel guilty for being mad and feeling sorry for herself because what if something horrible had happened.

But nothing horrible ever happened to her men. They just always went MIA because they craved freedom from Tania's coddling. And no, this is not a relationship, not even close, and of course Tania gets all that. But forgive her for not proclaiming her joy from the rooftops at the first sight of Ryan this morning. In fact, a part of her is a little crushed that he looks perfectly fine. Which means he just chose to disappear without a reason.

'Hey, I'm really sorry about disappearing like that,' Ryan says as if on cue when Tania bends down to greet Virus without saying a word to him. 'One of those personal emergencies,' he adds. This somehow makes Tania even more upset because now he was clearly drawing boundaries by using the word 'personal', and Tania hates boundaries especially with people whose faces she's awkwardly held under a coconut tree in full public view. And besides, this palpable sense of something bigger brewing beneath the surface has been there throughout their two-month relationship which involved two long coffee dates (which weren't acknowledged as dates, of course) apart from their daily training sessions where personal boundaries were blurred. And now it seems as though she's the only one who's felt any of it.

She buries her face a second longer in Virus' golden coat while she prepares her breezy queen face. It's difficult though. Tania has always been the poster child for the Myers–Briggs Feeling type. She tends to wear her emotions on her sleeve, but she can't have Ryan think she's upset with him for disappearing. No way. That would be embarrassingly premature, and he might think she's crazy. It's a different matter that she is. But it's polite to wait until you know someone for at least six months before you unleash your crazy on them. This is really more about politeness than self-preservation.

'Oh, it's totally fine,' Tania says, half-meeting his eyes. 'I wasn't able to make it a couple of days myself but figured you'd understand.'

'Oh, everything okay?' Ryan says.

'Yeah, yeah. Just had a cold. You?'

'I'm great,' he says it too quickly like she'd find out he's lying if he lingered on the word any longer. She finds out anyway. Tania has a borderline supernatural radar for these things. What people say versus what they don't say and sometimes, what they don't yet know. The only problem is when she lets her personal feelings get in the way and that's when anxiety takes over. Her intuition is usually quite spot-on.

'Okay,' Tania says and makes a mental note: *Discomfort with the emotional realm, probably a thinking type like Meg.*

'So, Virus, do you remember all the commands we learnt?' And with that, she turns her full attention to Virus and decidedly avoids such things as lingering eye contact, meaningful smiles and pretty much any kind of verbal exchange with Ryan.

'Are you sure everything's okay?' Ryan asks an hour later as they're about to wind up. 'You just look...I don't know...out of it.' Is he kidding? He just disappears on our girl after the weird face-holding, doesn't have the courtesy to acknowledge it (awkward as it may be) but then, has the audacity to keep asking if she's alright? Could people really live in so much denial?

Tania smiles vaguely.

'I'm not particularly good at this stuff but this is just me letting you know that if you want to talk...about anything...'

This somehow breaks through her breezy queen face. It must have taken so much for him to say this. He's clearly very bad at expressing himself emotionally so it's the effort that counts for Tania. 'I was a little worried about your disappearance, is all...'

'Worried?'

'Yeah, I'm an anxious wreck and I worry when my people disappear...I worry that something happened to them...I know, it's completely absurd, I should get treatm...'

'No, it's not absurd – it's sweet.' He appears genuinely moved. Like there's much more he wants to say but has no idea how.

Tania smiles. 'Well, I should probably get going,' she says at last and regrets it immediately after. She was just giving him a way out of a conversation that was clearly making him uncomfortable. But what if she was wrong? What if he was about to say things and she stopped him?

'Uh, yes, yes, of course…' Ryan stutters a bit. 'Thank you,' he says, making the most intense eye contact he's made with her so far. She can tell it's a lot bigger than 'thank you for training my dog'. It's more along the lines of 'Thank you for holding my face, sorry I'm such a coward, and if you can still find it in you to forgive me and give me some time, I'd really appreciate that.'

'You're welcome,' Tania says but realizes she's the one having trouble maintaining eye contact this time.

'Oh, and if you'd let me have your number, I can let you know in case of another emergency,' Ryan says, and Tania's heart starts to make its existence felt.

They exchange numbers and say goodbye and the rest of Tania's day disappears in a '90s romantic ballad.

'So grateful for today' Tania makes note in her intention journal. *'Thank you, Universe.'*

Things I want to work on before we get to Capricorn season:

- *Quit blaming myself for what are obviously other people's issues*
- *Work on setting and maintaining boundaries*
- *Become self-contained without losing my Cancerian ability to nurture and be receptive to nurturing from others*

~

'See, this is why I'm beginning to think the arranged marriage route is better,' Meg says when Tania relates the big happenings of the day.

'Meghana Rao, advocate for arranged marriage… *Wow*! The world must be coming to an end.'

'No, I just mean this endless waiting and wondering and reading between the lines and having anxiety attacks about being liked and liked enough...it's exhausting! Not to mention insulting and demeaning and...anyway... I just had to respond to a profile on a matrimonial website, and we've been texting like teenagers since. No wasting time. Works for me!'

'Yes, I'm working on my anxiety. But the whole point of falling in love is knowing everything that you're risking by putting yourself out there, is worth it and finding out that you were right to do it! It's high stakes and therefore, gratifying!'

'Sure, except here, I write to a guy who has clearly stated he's single and looking, I appear to match the qualities he's looking for in a mate and vice versa, and we make contact knowing that a) there's very little room for rejection, and b) should rejection still occur, who the fuck cares?'

'So romantic,' Tania says.

'See, that's the point. It's not about the romance. It's about the fastest, least turbulent route to the destination.' Meg leans back smugly on the sofa and takes a big sip of her coffee.

19

'Maybe becoming your mother isn't the worst thing that could happen.' – Meg

Rajeev Menon hasn't even appeared in the flesh yet but he's already triggered the most fascinating transformation in Meg's relationship with her mother. With concrete progress being made with Rajeev, a respectable architect as opposed to a musician still waiting for his big break, it feels like lifelong barriers in their mother–daughter relationship have magically fallen away. In fact, Meg is currently lazing in bed at her mother's place while her mother is in the kitchen, insisting on making every one of Meg's childhood favourites. Of course, when she was a child, it was her grandmother who was doing the cooking. In fact, her mother had barely been around to even notice if she ate anything, let alone pay any attention to *what* she had eaten. At least that's how it appeared to eight-year-old Meg who had learnt to replace Mom with 'Ammamma'. But now, over the last two days that she's been lounging at her mother's place, she's changed her mind. Maybe she had seen it all wrong. Maybe her mother had in fact been nurturing, but she had been too blinded by her attachment to her grandmother to realize. How else could she explain her mum turning into another person literally overnight? It did not make sense. These things did *not* happen in Meg's world.

'I know you've always thought that I put my work and friends before you, and you're not wrong to suppose that. But you have to understand that someone had to be the responsible one in the family with your dad being...your dad. The few friends I had were my only support system,' Kavitha says in a confessional moment that catches Meg by surprise. Was she reading her mind? Given how Meg's father had abandoned them, had Kavitha been any less stoic, she'd have completely come undone considering how much harder it had been to be a working single mother in those days.

'I know, Mom,' Meg says. She's moved by this genuine display of emotion even as it makes her extremely uncomfortable. Heart-to-hearts are not a thing with her mother. She preferred to keep the conversation strictly about practical matters. But maybe that's changing now and it's easy to understand why. Meg is finally making the choice Kavitha always wished she'd made instead of running away and marrying Meg's father. 'I know you did the best you could.'

Kavitha smiles. 'You know, one of the most painful experiences as a parent is to watch your child make the same mistakes you made. It's unbearable. So many times, as I watched you grow up, I wished you'd be smarter than I was. And I know I didn't handle that well, but that's because I felt guilty. How would you know what choices to make when I'd never been there for you? You were raised by my mother, god bless her, but she was a simple woman. She couldn't have warned you about the kind of men you'd meet and must avoid. But somehow, I couldn't either. The guilt of not being there for you and having missed out on your childhood was all just too overwhelming.' Her voice grows thin as her eyes well up and Meg, who is beyond amazed at this, hesitantly reaches out to hold her hand. 'Anyway,' Kavitha says, pulling herself together, 'I'm glad you're finally making the right choice. Rajeev seems perfect,' she smiles approvingly.

Meg smiles back. 'Well, thank you for picking him out for me.'

'You and I aren't very different, you know,' Kavitha says.

'So, I'm usually told,' Meg says. Tania and Neel have always had this opinion, and it always led to a fight. But now in this oddly personal exchange with her mother, she finally sees it.

'So, tell me more about Rajeev. When do I get to meet him?'

'Mom, I haven't met him yet!' Meg reminds her.

'We must quickly fix that. He lives in Bangalore, which is basically next door…'

'Actually, he's in Singapore now and going to be there for a while,' Meg says.

'Okay, so that's not next door but it's two streets away.'

Meg laughs. 'Yes, but I don't want to be the one to suggest it. I'm sure he'll bring it up when he's ready or when he's less busy with work.' The truth is, Meg isn't ready yet. She's come this far and it's been fun, but meeting the guy would make it real.

'You've at least Skyped him, no? Seen his face in good light? Sometimes they look nothing like the photograph!' This is a serious question.

'Yes, Mom, I've Skyped him several times and he is even better on video,' Meg says blushing a little.

'Okay, fine. Let me also Skype him. You would have had at least three or four sessions with him by now, no?'

Meg has had a lot more than three or four 'sessions' but something in her protests this. She really doesn't think it's a good idea to introduce her mother to Rajeev yet. She has a tendency to be intrusive and not recognize it as intrusion. Although that just might be an Indian parent thing. Her phone buzzes as if on cue. It's Rajeev.

'See? The universe agrees!' Kavitha says. 'Ask him to get on Skype and meet the parent!'

Meg rolls her eyes. 'You sound like Tania.' But she relents and introduces the two. To her surprise, Rajeev totally charms her mother. He's *that* guy. The one that mothers adore. This is all very new for Meg who is so used to being chided – both in her own head and outside – for being irresponsible and dating musicians without jobs. *Is this for real?* Meg wonders as she steps into the shower. *Not only am I very close to winning the bet but I'm also bonding with my mom and making major psychological progress to boot?*

20

'Maybe closed doors are just as valid a sign as open doors. They tell you where you shouldn't go.' – Tania

'What do you think?' Tania is trying to find the right outfit for her big date with Ryan. Well, it's a 'Thank you for training Virus' dinner if we're using his words but in Tania's head, it's Ryan's code for a date because he's awkward and does not know how to ask a woman out.

'You looked fine four changes ago,' Meg says, cloaking her strong disapproval of this 'date' in general disinterest.

'Well, fine isn't good enough,' Tania marches off into the bedroom to find yet another dress. The dinner is still a couple of hours away, but she's got other grooming matters to attend to. 'Would "fine" do if you were meeting Rajeev or if it was your first opportunity to let Rajeev see you in something other than track pants?' she calls out from the bedroom.

'Right, because my clear equation with Rajeev and this brain fog you have going with Ryan are *exactly* the same thing,' Meg cannot stop herself from saying. She's usually a believer in tough love and letting people burn their fingers in order for the lesson to sink in. But it must be all that bonding with her mother, because she's feeling nauseatingly protective of Tania and exasperated that Tania can't see this.

'That's harsh,' Tania has returned, wearing yet another date outfit. 'There's no fog. It's called going with the flow.'

'Then why, after,' Meg pauses to check the calendar, 'more than three months of knowing him and meeting him almost every single day, do you still not know if he's single?'

'I don't know! It hasn't come up,' Tania says.

Meg cannot believe she's having this conversation. 'How can it not come up? You clearly think there is palpable chemistry between you two, and you say you have a strong emotional bond and you've bartered stories about your childhood and parents and first loves. So how, pray tell, can it not come up?'

'Because I haven't asked him. Okay? *God*.' Meg's newfound maternal instinct is clearly triggering Tania's rebellious teenager instinct.

'Why not?'

'Because he's the kind of person who has clear boundaries. Know people like that? Oh, wait. *You*. That's right, he's the kind of stubborn person who will not be persuaded into discussing anything until he is actually ready. And I can tell that so far, this is a box he does not wish to open.'

'And doesn't that tell you everything you need to know?' Meg is relentless. She can see Tania is about to break, and she hates spoiling this big date for her but she's quite sure it's going to end in disappointment.

Tania walks out of the conversation and locks herself in her room till it's time to leave.

'Tan, I'm just watching out for you,' Meg calls out through the door.

Tania switches her blow dryer on in response.

~

It's 8.30 p.m. and Ryan is waiting for her outside Smokey's, the cozy little neighbourhood pizza place a couple of streets away from Raintree where they're actually headed. This had seemed cute to Tania when he had suggested it – it had a distinct '90s vibe about it. But now it appears shady because…well, this is not the '90s and they are not teenagers sneaking out and…oh my god! Is Meg right and is this the Neptune fog that astrologers keep warning you about? The one where you see things that are not there? Her house is right here! Why couldn't he come over and ring the fucking bell?

What is going on with this ostensible non-date date. 'Hush,' Tania tells herself. 'You can't go in feeling like this.' One look at her perfectly manicured nails, hair painstakingly set into good behaviour mode for nearly 45 minutes and the endless wardrobe changes before arriving at this one – a strappy black dress that she had always avoided wearing because it was always 'too glamorous for this occasion', with a thin, beige shawl thrown over it so as to tone down the glamour while giving it a more effortlessly elegant appeal – and Tania starts to feel stupid again for being the first one to jump off another cliff while the other party is still undecided.

'Hey…' Ryan says and forgets the rest of his sentence rather dramatically as he realizes how different she looks when she's not in tracks and has hair serum in, and this makes him subconsciously reach for his own hair in a halfway self-conscious manner.

Tania notices this and immediately feels better. The very real conflict she experienced just a few seconds ago is entirely cancelled out. No guy who was emotionally invested in another relationship would let himself look at her like that. And so openly. This is, of course, Tania logic but she doesn't let herself be bothered by that. Right now, all that matters is that she is right and Meg is wrong and that this just might be her breakthrough night where she gets him to admit something of his feelings for her. She needs to know. Also, she's looking forward to Ryan after a few drinks. He's totally the kind of guy who could use some loosening up.

'You ready?' Ryan says at last and instinctively reaches for her hand but awkwardly pulls away – but only after setting off some legitimate sparks from the accidental brush of hands. Tania notices this because, well, it's hard not to when Uranus shows up as an attractive man sending lightning bolts through your body. They walk slowly, Tania's heels a good excuse to not rush, hands 'accidentally' brushing up against each other's a couple more times to check if the lightning bolts were a one-time thing (spoiler: they are not). Tania directs all her focus on making her very real blushing pass off as smiling, and Ryan directs all his focus on pretending not to notice this while thoroughly revelling in the moment.

The bar is mostly empty since it's a weeknight and because it's no longer the coolest place in town. Tania had picked this one quite deliberately. She really didn't want one of those noisy places filled with drunk young people and loud music getting in the way of any meaningful conversation.

'What am I having?' Tania surveys the menu like an excited child. 'Mmm...I'm in an adventurous mood, so I think I'll have the weird cocktail with the red chilli in it.' Ryan watches her like everything about her is adorable and surprising. 'You know what you want?' she asks him, seeing as he's not even opened his menu.

'I always know what I want,' he smiles. *Ooh.*

'So what will it be? Let me guess. You look like a bourbon kind of guy.' Tania flashes one of her most charming smiles.

'Yeah, I'm fairly predictable like that,' Ryan smiles. 'But I'm not drinking tonight.'

Tania is crestfallen and it's obvious. She had counted on alcohol bringing his walls down tonight. It also strikes her as particularly depressing that he wouldn't drink on the one night he goes out with her. This must just be his way of making it crystal clear that this is not a date. And suddenly all her doubts start to rise up again, combined with Meg's warnings about brain fog, and Tania is dangerously close to exploding.

'Why not?' she asks.

'Well, weeknight…' he drawls.

He doesn't really have an answer she notes. And now she's definitely upset. 'Then why would you come to a bar on a weeknight if you weren't planning on drinking?' she tries to sound calm, but her irritation is visible.

'Because I wanted it to be a place you like, and you picked this one,' Ryan's matter-of-factness is even more infuriating than his general vagueness at this point.

'Well I don't drink alone – maybe we should just go home,' Tania says, closing the menu.

'Come on,' Ryan says. 'Have a drink and you'll feel better.' He's saying all the wrong things.

That's it. That's the trigger. 'I don't need to feel better, Ryan. I need answers. Now I know you're going to pretend like you don't understand what I'm saying, and you might even make me feel delusional but I don't care. I can't deal with the vagueness anymore!'

'Ohh-kay, slow down. What are you talking about?'

'I'm talking about the emotional iceberg between us that you never want to discuss. I'm talking about how I've felt a distinct sense of belonging since we first met, and the way I feel when you're not quite connected to me. The deep closeness I feel with you that I can't seem to explain to anyone or myself because I have no idea what we're doing here, and for all I know you could be some married creep…'

Ryan watches her with a pained expression in his face that you can't really read.

'I'm talking about how I've fallen in love with you over the last three months and have no idea where I stand with you. It's painful and humiliating.' Her voice breaks and something inside Ryan's chest seems to snap and give way too but there is no visible sign of this except for the pained expression on his face growing more intense, the silence even louder, making Tania swing from expectant to heartbroken in a few minutes.

Ryan doesn't say anything – his deep sense of inadequacy about meeting the emotional needs of others, is triggered by Tania's display of hurt and disappointment in him. It quickly sucks him into a vortex of old pain and rejection that have nothing to do with Tania, as these emotional situations often do. When he finally opens his mouth to speak, it is to order a drink. He clearly needs it.

'You're just not going to say anything, are you?' Tania says after a few minutes of this excruciating, heartbreaking silence. Hot, fat tears fall from her large, kohl-lined eyes, making her feel weak and pathetic.

'I don't know what to say,' Ryan says and looks like he's about to cry too.

'Well, that's an answer,' and with that Tania picks up her things and walks out, leaving Ryan alone to have his bourbon.

21

'A gut feeling is a myth invented by someone who couldn't think.' - Meg

It has been a couple of weeks since Rajeev's meet-the-parent Skype call and Meg is feeling rather upbeat these days. She has a totally workable potential relationship in her hands (potential only because Meg refuses to acknowledge any bonds forged over the phone or Internet as 'real'), a loving relationship with her mother (something she never thought she missed), and Rajeev has finally committed to an actual date. He'll be flying down to see her in a fortnight! And though a nagging irritation in the pit of her stomach accompanies this general sense of positivity, Meg is well-trained at not paying attention to her feelings. Especially those that originate in the gut. They are vague and entirely useless, and Meg does not need more uselessness in her life.

What she needs now is Tania. Her friend, her shadow, her cheerleader. It's painful to not be able to share this news with her, but Tania is too busy moping, being upset with Ryan, herself and the universe! She's still replaying their conversation from a week ago in her head to find something that might excuse his behaviour. Something that would allow her to continue to believe in the connection she thought she had with him, in the electric currents that surged through her body during that bizarre face-holding and then the walk to the bar, even if nothing had come of it. Right now, he just seems like a spineless douche who wants her attention but is clearly married, or for whatever reason, does not want to be with her or even be seen with her (hence, the weeknight non-date).

'Please stop doing this to yourself,' Meg says, bringing Tania some tea. 'You're acting like this is a major break up.'

Tania says nothing and that's always ominous.

'Okay, it *was* a break up,' Meg concedes. 'I don't get it, but I get that that's how it probably feels like for you because you're so intense...'

Tania stares listlessly out of the bedroom window.

Meg sighs heavily and turns around to leave since Tania is clearly in no mood to chat.

'I know it doesn't make any sense, but I still believe that I was right about what we had. He's the one who's lying. He's the one who's pretending nothing ever happened. And I'm just pissed off that I can't prove it – and not feeling sad and pathetic like I used to when I was younger,' Tania says, still staring out the window.

Meg is moved by this insight and is baffled by the fact that she is. This newfound mother love is clearly softening her edges. 'I'm sorry, Tan. But I'm glad you found out now rather than later, you know?'

'See, that's the thing!' Tania says, finally turning around to face her. 'I haven't found anything! I still don't know the real reason behind his silence and this mystery. What if I'm right and it was all real? Maybe he has a good reason...'

'Please don't go there!' Meg cannot believe Tania's optimism at times.

'What if he's going through some kind of relationship-related

PTSD? What if he had a wife but she died? What if the real story is dark and tragic and he wasn't quite ready to share it.'

'Oh, for the love of god, listen to yourself!' Meg yells without intending to, but Tania isn't listening anymore. She's managed to convince herself that this is the explanation. This has to be it. Because the relationship itself is real. There's some darkness holding Ryan back and only true love's kiss can save him from it. She must get to the bottom of this.

'I have to know for sure, Meg. I can't let it go until I know.' Tania says with the resolve of a fairy-tale princess.

'And how do you plan on investigating?' Meg asks. 'Since you said it yourself – Ryan is not someone who can be persuaded into talking about anything unless he wants to.'

'Yes but I was harsh the other night. I walked out on him. Not that he didn't deserve it. But knowing how conflict-averse he is, he's probably afraid of talking to me now.'

'Right, *that's* why he's been texting you nonstop since that night, trying to find a way to get through.' Meg is no longer feeling tender and maternal. Someone needed to point out Tania's stupidities to her, and who better to do it than Meg.

Tania doesn't have anything to say to this. It's a good point. If any of this was real and Ryan really did have a genuine reason, he would have at least texted her by now. Texts are as non-confrontational as it gets. But there's been nothing. And there really is no excuse for it. Tania dissolves into a fresh bout of disappointment this time. She's exhausted from repeatedly pulling herself out of her despair by stitching together elaborate excuses for Ryan only for it all to come unravelling by a single reasonable question. When will she learn to take things at face value and stop seeing the story from the other person's point of view?

'You know what,' she says after a minute of quiet consideration.

'I'm done figuring it out. I'm done figuring him out. I have a life, a business to run, a partner who needs me, and a psycho client who needs to be contained. I'm done moping.'

Meg smiles her fullest smile. 'That's my girl!'

Tania throws her wardrobe open and proceeds to pull out her power suit for a new day with Meera Anand.

'And hey,' Meg says. 'Is this a really bad time to tell you that Rajeev is coming down to see me in a couple of weeks?'

'Whaaaaat?' Tania is squealing in delight and jumping up and down like she wasn't completely devastated just minutes ago. 'You let me whine about Ryan all this time while you kept this from me? Why?'

Meg grins. 'I don't know how you do that, but I'm glad you do.'

22

'Sometimes, shit happens for no fathomable reason. It's like the universe is having a bad day.' – Tania

The background music in Meg's head has changed from the blues to something upbeat and cheery because she's this close to meeting her...goal. Yes, goal. Let there be no illusions about romance and fluttering hearts, please. This is all about the rush that comes from beginning a project (in this case, finding love) and accomplishing it. Nevertheless, the very real progress in her relationship with Rajeev is helping in no small measure with office politics and the quietly raging cold war with Hiten.

Actually, there is no war. Hiten is a lot of things but he isn't spiteful and petty. If he's being petty, Meg gets all the credit for it. Her unconscious competitiveness and the need to always win creates rivals for her wherever she goes.

Not to mention how this situation has also been working as an excellent distraction from all the emotional energy flowing by default in Neel's direction. Meg hates that. The thought that emotional energy can just flow in a direction that she doesn't intend, or want, is enough to keep her up at night. If it takes an artificially created rival to play out this drama in her head so that she can stay focused on the everyday pettiness as opposed to the intense feelings for her ex, then so be it.

'You seem chipper,' Hiten says as Meg skips into the room. Yes, she skips in like a gleeful five year old.

'Don't sound so surprised. I'm happy! I'm a happy person!' Meg makes herself coffee and makes a mental note to never skip again, no matter how excited she is about meeting Rajeev... err...the Goal.

'Then let me make you even happier and tell you that you are in charge of putting together a launch event for Red Dot W&P!'

'What–?'

'...in two weeks!'

'What, no wa–'

'It's happening, Meg. The team from London's coming down, the entire office seems to think that you're the only one who can pull it off and so I'm kind of counting on you.' Hiten has learnt a thing or two about what drives Meg and is willing to use it in these petty games. See, Meg absolutely hates organizing parties. That's her least favourite thing. But she also cannot turn down a challenge. Especially one where everyone's counting on her. It's a win-win for Hiten who was originally assigned the job and who knows only too well that it's next to impossible to pull off the kind of party that the W&P team is expecting in two weeks.

'I guess I'm organizing the launch party in two weeks then,' Meg says to an empty room sipping her coffee.

'Thanks, Meg!' Hiten calls out from the adjoining room. 'Will send you an email with the list.'

The list? What list? Meg is not used to ticking off to-do items from other people's lists. *She's* the list maker. That is how it works! But no one's listening, and an email is on its way to her inbox with more details than she can keep up with, including a fun fact: the party coincides with the day Rajeev is coming down. Of course, Meg doesn't know that yet, and so the panic attack can wait.

~

Meanwhile, at Ever After, Tania is dealing with something quite similar – except she has no idea what it is. She can tell she's coming down with something. But she feels quite all right physically. The Ryan episode still hurts, but it's only been a couple of weeks and she's giving it time. This is something else. This is foreboding. But then again, she's been reading all those articles on Uranus opposing her Venus and how it often leads to love at first sight and other unexpected scenarios on the love front only to end in sudden and unexpected disappointment. But that's already happened. This has got to be something else. Maybe it's Meera. Maybe she has a whole new tantrum planned for the day. But what's so unexpected about that?

Her phone buzzes. It's a text from Aditi.

`Cannot begin to tell you how thankful I am that you're doing this all by yourself. I owe you big time.`

And that's the other thing. Aditi's young and recently laid-off husband has had a mild stroke and is in the hospital. Things have hit an all-time low for poor Aditi. She now, more than ever, needs this Meera wedding to go off smoothly.

'Maybe it's just that,' Tania tells herself. 'I'm worried about screwing this up for Aditi!'

She starts to type a comforting text to Aditi but is interrupted by Meera making a dramatic entrance, clapping her hands and calling out her name as if summoning her minion. There is a young woman with her and if not for her striking resemblance to Meera, Tania would've never thought this was the bride, Shruti.

There's just something about Shruti – perhaps it's her straight hair in a casual bun, her nose ring, complete lack of make-up except for heavily kohl-lined eyes, unthreaded eyebrows and upper lip that make her look oddly attractive, her being dressed in jeans and a T-shirt that says www.freethegirlchild.org – she is the picture of a passionate activist type who's dealing with too many issues of global importance to have any time for something as pointless and conventional as a wedding. But then again, we're inside Tania's imagination now, and we all know it's a colourful place.

'Put your phone down and greet the bride already,' Meera barks at her, making herself comfortable on Aditi's chair.

'I apologize for everything she's making you do and undo, and for how she generally is,' Shruti says, coming forward to meet Tania. 'I'm Shruti,' she smiles. It's a natural, genuine smile that instantly endears her to Tania. It's almost impossible to believe she could be related to Meera.

'I've been looking forward to meeting you, Shruti,' Tania says. 'Wish Aditi were here too. She's caught up at home but she would've loved to meet you too and...'

'What is more important than meeting her highest-paying client on a Tuesday morning?' Meera interrupts.

'Her husband had a stroke and is in the hospital,' Tania says curtly out of habit and immediately worries that she's letting Aditi down by being herself.

'I am so sorry,' Shruti says and Tania hears the sincerity in her tone. 'Again, I apologize for my sister.'

Meera rolls her eyes.

'So...shall we get on with it then?' Tania says, limiting her smiles and eye contact to Shruti.

'Yeah, not yet,' Meera butts in. 'We're waiting for Mister Way-Below-Her-League-And-Can't-Make-It-To-Anything-

On-Time.'

'Meera, can you NOT…' Shruti is at the verge of snapping at her sister in front of Tania when Mister Way-Below-Her-League aka Shruti's fiancé enters and Tania has trouble swallowing. And thinking. And breathing.

It's Ryan. Of course. Because the universe just doesn't go to the trouble of organizing a Venus–Uranus opposition without delivering the goods. But it doesn't make any sense. The groom's name is Ashwin. Which makes this all so much worse. Ryan was not only engaged all along but he wasn't even Ryan?

The rest of the meeting is a blur for Tania, who only manages to survive the palpitations by excusing herself to the restroom, drinking lots of water and giving herself a long lecture on how much Aditi needs her to keep this going. If Ryan is also having a similar reaction, there is no way of knowing since Tania is hell-bent on not meeting his eyes. At least not through this meeting. Thankfully, Shruti gets a call and has to leave and since Meera cannot imagine being in the same room with Ryan, the meeting is mercifully cut short, and Tania is on her way home where she can proceed to throw up the contents of her breakfast in peace.

Back home, Nandu and Meenakshi Aunty see Tania walking in and call out from their balconies. 'Is it true? Meg is winning? Is a Singapore-architect boy coming down to meet her?' How they know is, as always, a mystery. 'This cannot happen. From this point on, we are taking over. We can win this bet for you! We…'

'Not now, Nandu,' Tania says and rushes into the house where she plans on hiding for the foreseeable future.

24

'Maybe in the end, I do not want to be proved right. Maybe I want the rainbows-and-unicorns people to win. But they just never do.' – Meg

Meg gets home from work after going through Hiten's absurd list of party requirements, only managing to maintain her poise by promising herself a hot shower and a bottle of wine. But at home she finds that Tania has already beaten her to it. In fact, the bottle is now nearly empty, and Tania is sprawled on the living room floor staring listlessly at the ceiling.

'No!' Meg cries. It feels like someone's sucker-punched her in the solar plexus. It's not about Tania finishing the wine. It's about the fact that this bottle of wine represented hope for Meg. It is all she had focused on all day when every fibre of her being wanted to barge into Hiten's office, stick a compass in his forehead (the seat of all ridiculous ideas) and staple his lips together (he'd have no way of opening them). Meg's violent fantasies almost always involved stationery. 'There is no way your day was worse than mine,' she says to Tania who doesn't seem to have noticed her. Meg walks around her like a dog sniffing a suspicious trail and finally sinks to the floor along with her bags. 'Okay, you've had a really bad couple of weeks, yes, but you survived it without wine. Surely Meera Anand couldn't have made you feel worse?'

'You want to play "Who Deserves All the Wine in the World?" 'Cause I'm winning.'

'I highly doubt that, but sure. Not that there is any wine left to play for.' Meg knows there's beer in the fridge, and normally she'd love a cold beer after a long day, but today, she needs hope. And all her hope had been magically transferred to that bottle of wine that Tania has just consumed. She picks up the bottle and takes a sip of what's left of it. 'Douchy Hiten is playing dirty with me. I have no choice but to endure it because I really need this job to be the stable thing in my life, like it's always been, while I pursue more important goals. So. A launch party needs to be organized for the company, the London team is going to be there and guess who's doing the honours? Yes. Me. Not only do I have to organize this stupid party, I have to source the most ridiculous list of must-haves for this party. Such as – wait for it – *Game of Thrones* themed ice sculptures. First, I don't know who makes ice sculptures in this city and second, I do not watch that stupid show. And if that isn't enough, the party is scheduled for the day I'm meeting Rajeev for dinner. And now I have to postpone that.'

Meg pauses for dramatic reflection and a response from Tania but it isn't forthcoming. 'Hello? Did you just hear what I said?'

'Ryan is the groom in the Meera Anand wedding,' Tania says, still staring at the ceiling.

'*WHAT?*' Meg spits out the only proper mouthful of wine she managed to get this evening. It seems the universe really didn't want Meg drinking any wine at all tonight. 'Are you... Oh my god... Wow... I mean...really...what the... Wow... I don't know what to say.'

'Yeah, I'm getting that sense,' Tania says dryly.

'Crap, I'm so sorry,' Meg says stretching herself on the floor next to Tania. 'I always worried that this would end in disappointment but I didn't see *this* coming. I'm so sorry, Tan.'

'Yeah.'

'Have you… do you know for sure or is this something you've put together?'

'I had no choice but to put it together when he walked into my office this morning with Meera and the bride and was introduced by both women as the groom.'

'Holy crap! This is like something out of *Grey's Anatomy*.'

'Except I will not be giving him 11 seasons of my life.'

But Meg is working the whole story out in her head and wants more details. 'Did you speak to him? Has he said anything?'

'He's been calling incessantly since the meeting and I haven't picked up.'

'Okay. But don't you want to talk to him? I mean, listen to his side of it?' Meg can't believe she's saying this. But this situation is so dramatic, it's hard to be rational.

'Are you kidding me?' Tania says. 'It's well past time for explanations. The only thing he owes me is not making me listen to his crappy excuse for being such a lying…coward.'

Meg sighs. 'Of course. What did Aditi say?'

'Aditi? Aditi doesn't know anything and doesn't need to. She has enough on her plate – she really needs me to come through for her on this. I mean, I promised her!'

'Tan, your being involved with the groom, even if you didn't know it, is kind of a big deal. Aditi is your partner and she deserves to know. I know I would want to know if I were in her shoes.'

'What is telling her going to achieve? It's going to make her anxious. She'd feel guilty for burdening me with seeing this through when I'd rather be running to the hills right about now. And I really want to be there for her. I promised her. I can't bail now because of boy drama of all things.'

'All very noble reasons. I'm just saying that if something goes wrong – maybe you can't take it anymore and you end up confronting him at work and someone gets a whiff of this and…'

'It won't happen.'

'I'm just saying it's better to tell…'

'It won't happen, Meg. And I'm not telling Aditi. Period.'

Two hours later, the two say goodnight and retire into their bedrooms. Meg is up worrying about how Tania is going to handle this situation and Tania is weeping into a pillow. 'I did everything right. I trusted the process, I went with my gut and the synchronicities. This was *supposed* to work!' she bawls. This feels like the cosmic equivalent of a long lecture and a tight slap, and what hurts most is not knowing the 'Why' and 'What now' of it because it leaves her with nothing to believe in anymore. As if on cue, her intention journal presses up against her neck from under her pillow. Tania opens it to a random page which just happens to be the entry about first meeting Ryan after being woken up by a voice. Copious tears flow on to the page, smudging the black ink, giving the pages a dark, ominous look. *This looks more like my life*, Tania wryly smiles through her tears.

25

'Relationships come with a best-before date and I assure you, Neel and I are way past ours.' – Meg

Meg is usually quite excellent at having things under control or at least appearing as though she does. But as the party-cum-meet-Rajeev date draws closer and closer, her ice queen façade begins to give way under the pressure. For starters, there is the obvious one: the party and the million things that can go wrong with it, especially at such short notice. But funnily, that's the least of Meg's concerns right now. She's more preoccupied with the possibility of not liking Rajeev in person – and the domino effect it would have on her new-found relationship with her mother. Let's not talk about how she'd be letting herself down if she doesn't meet her goal for the year. But there's an unconscious preoccupation as well and one that's far more worrying simply because it's unconscious: Neel. Our heroine is not over her ex and doesn't know it. As far as she's concerned, they're 'just feelings' that surface every now and then and must be shown the door because her mind would be a lot better occupied with the Goal. Curiously, Meg does not know a whole lot about how the unconscious operates with an agenda of its own.

And since so much of her preoccupation is happening at a

different level of her psyche, it manifests as incessant heartburn and headaches. 'That's new,' Meg mutters to herself as she makes her way through the parking lot of the nearest mall, carrying more party supplies than she is comfortable being seen with. 'I usually never get heartburn when I'm stressed –' She's bumped into someone. 'Owww! Watch it!' she says as a matter of habit, though it is entirely her fault. The gentleman apologizes also out of habit. It's Neel. This is the first time they're running into each other (literally) post the break up.

'Meg!' Neel greets her with his signature dimple-flashing, heart-stopping, Bollywood hero smile and Meg is a touch unprepared to see him this happy and it shows. A little. For a second, it feels like those repressed feelings, personified as Neel, have come back for revenge, and she can't be in denial anymore. This is all too sudden and frightening for Meg, who can handle just about any confrontation except the emotional kind. 'Crap,' she says as she struggles to find the words. A knot in her chest warns her that if she doesn't flee the scene, this story could go a whole other way with consequences she can't afford.

'Ohh-kay, it's great to see you too,' Neel smiles again in case he hadn't made his point earlier.

'No…no, no…I'm just…late!' Not letting anyone catch her having an emotional moment is one of Meg's key defences, and she says the first thing that comes to mind before Neel sees her unravel right there. She's put months into convincing herself that she doesn't miss him and is, in fact, quite over him. The threat of having all those repressed emotions rushing back at once is too much to handle for any self-respecting ice queen.

'Right. Okay. I won't hold you up.' He's still smiling, though not as fully anymore.

'Right…bye,' Meg says and starts to walk towards her car about ten feet away but stops in her tracks. *What if this is a good thing*, she wonders. Perhaps this is one of those meaningful coincidences that Tania is always talking about. An opportunity for closure! And the timing is perfect too, with Rajeev coming down in a week. She turns around tentatively to see how far he's gone but Neel is still there, as if he's been waiting for her to turn around. And just for those few seconds, Meg is completely in love with him again. But she remembers that he's a musician still living with his parents, driving his friend's car and waiting for his big break and the inner poise returns.

'How are you?' she says at last.

'I'm good. I've a job, you know?'

'Is that right?' Meg is genuinely surprised.

'And one that I'm actually enjoying.'

'Wait…you didn't…'

'Yes I did,' Neel grins. Meg had always told him she could see him as a top chef – the kind that appeared on TV shows – but Neel had no plans of pursuing his culinary career beyond college because music had always come first and he somehow imagined he'd stop playing if he had a job that he loved. 'I'm working at The Cove with Sanjay Menon!'

The mention of 'Menon' makes Meg's insides hurt as she remembers that she has a big date next week with a man who is not Neel. 'I'm really happy for you,' she says sincerely but Neel being extra perceptive when it comes to Meg, detects the hint of ambivalence in her tone.

'We can still make this work, Meg,' he says, stepping closer and taking hold of both her hands in his. 'I wanted to wait till I was a little more settled before I told you 'cause I didn't want to make another empty promise...'

'No, Neel, this isn't about me. This is all you… this is…'

'Of course it's about you! You think I would have moved my ass and taken the whole parallel career thing seriously otherwise? And you haven't even heard the best parts yet! I love the job, I'm extremely good at it, *and* we're finally releasing our first album early next year, *and* I've moved out!

This is all a bit much for Meg to take in in one sitting. Or standing. Also, it's just like Neel to pick the most inconvenient of spots for grand confessions. They're in the middle of a parking lot, she's still holding bags of party supplies and there are vehicles honking at them. 'Let's move to the side,' she says, and they stop at the corner where her car is parked. Meg wants to say a lot of things, express all the emotions that want to emerge but she's afraid of saying too much. What does this all mean and why, *why*, should she listen to this now? What if this is the universe's way of stopping her from meeting Rajeev? What if the whole Rajeev thing is a really bad idea that's going to blow up in her face? These are questions that Tania may have asked, but Meg being Meg immediately dismisses any suggestion of 'the universe', swallows everything she wants to say, puts on her ice queen face and says, 'I'm really happy for you, Neel. But I have moved on and you should too.'

'What?' Neel doesn't believe a word. 'What do you mean I should move on? I can't move on from you. And neither should you. When it's real, you make it work because you *can't* move on.' He was always hot when he was intense, but Meg really needs to get away from him before she lets him infect her with the same feelings.

'I'm sorry,' she says as she tears away from him, gets into her car and drives away like someone who does not wish to be pursued by the past.

Once home, Meg skips her coffee (the last thing she needs

right now is an over-stimulated mind), climbs into bed and opens her journal. It feels like one of those nights when she could stay up all night writing. And the thought is terrifying. The last thing she wants to do is make those feelings conscious by describing them in words. She slams the journal shut like it's a horror novel she never wants to read, turns off the lights and wills all her focus into counting sheep.

26

'We like to imagine that our love lives will play out like romcoms, but maybe they're more like a sad Nicholas Sparks novel and instead of somebody dying on you, you end up running your car over them or something out of sheer rage.' – Tania

Planning the wedding of a man you were in love with a week ago can be a bit of a challenge as Tania is realizing. Especially if said man has unfinished business with you and is hell-bent on fixing that. But Tania is letting her rage fuel her determination to avoid him at all costs and is doing a pretty impressive job except for the fact that Ryan, who by the way, is Ryan – it's his middle name though, the name his mother gave him and the one he identified with strongly, even more so after she passed away when he was still a young child (not that any of this has made Tania soften up to him, to her credit) – is always one step ahead. Like today, when he decided to go with Meera and her for wedding band auditions. (The bride had to be somewhere more important – something about refugee children and online teaching commitments). Tania is at her wit's end with Ryan who clearly can't seem to take a hint. Besides, where was all this courage just a couple of weeks ago when she basically begged him for an explanation?

'You really need to stop,' Tania whispers to Ryan the minute she gets a chance. Meera is on the stage, giving jazz lessons to unsuspecting jazz musicians. 'This wedding is the only thing I've got right now, and I need it to go well. It's difficult enough without my partner around, with Meera being Meera and the fact that it's *your* wedding that I'm planning – I don't need you to make it worse and let Meera sniff out something that doesn't even exist in the first place,' she blurts it all out in one breath.

'Tania…' Ryan says and for a second, she melts. The way he says her name is just so…right. 'I cannot even imagine what you're going through…'

'Yeah? Well, anger, confusion, rage, betrayal and devastation should just about cover it.'

'Look,' Ryan speaks quickly seeing that Meera is about to get off the stage. 'I don't have much time and I need to talk to you. Just trust me this one last time and let me talk to you 'cause it's important and I want you to be the first to know this time.'

'What are you two bickering about?' Meera says taking her seat between them and Tania freezes for a moment. She hadn't realized Meera was right behind her for a second.

'I was telling Tania that I don't even like jazz,' Ryan says casually like he isn't, in fact, dealing with Medusa.

'And that's why nobody consults the groom when it comes to weddings. And I mean grooms who are actually equal partners to the bride…'

This keeps them bickering for a while and Tania is relieved to note that she had frozen over nothing. But still. This is all getting a bit out of hand. Just like Meg had said. Maybe she is biting off more than she can chew. But there is no choice. Aditi's life has hit a real low point. There is no way Tania can tell her. Not now. But what's Ryan on about? What is this important thing she should know before anyone else? What if he's planning on telling Shruti about her and calling off the wedding? She couldn't possibly live that down. Not to mention what would happen to her friendship with Aditi and their business, which is still in its teething stages. Too much drama. How easy they make it look in romcoms where the lead characters are willing to abandon everything for love!

Tania had always wanted that sort of high stakes experience when it came to love but now that it's so close to becoming her reality, it's the last thing she wants. She is not ready to risk everything that she's built in her life for the sake of love – true or not. Strange as it sounds, she really wishes Shruti were here. It would be so much easier to plan this with her. But Tania smells something off about this entirely loveable bride. Sure, she's someone who runs an NGO and cares more about children in Afghanistan than picking out wedding clothes, which is really all right. But there's a pronounced indifference to the wedding itself. *Maybe she doesn't want to be in this either*, Tania finds herself thinking.

'And wouldn't that be really convenient?' Meg's voice in the back of her mind snaps her out of her reverie. Ryan and Meera are still bickering, and Tania senses that this is the moment to escape. 'Guys, I have to run. It's a medical emergency,' she lies. 'I hope you two don't need me right now?'

'Please take him with you,' Meera says.

'Is everything okay?' Ryan says. You can tell he doesn't quite believe this medical emergency excuse but then again, her partner's husband did just have a stroke.

'Yeah, it's just Aditi. I'll be fine,' Tania says. 'Meera, maybe you could text me once you've decided on the band? That's the final thing I need a decision on. I'll be able to take it from there.'

'Done,' Meera says, already distracted by the next band.

Tania feels a sharp relief in her chest as she reaches the parking lot. Being in such close proximity to Ryan was more painful than she had imagined. She cannot afford to let that happen again. She's just going to have to find an alternative to working with him directly that doesn't involve Aditi finding out about any of this. Her phone rings as if on cue. It's her mother.

'Hmm,' Tania smiles. 'Maybe it's time to run to the hills after all.'

27

'I read somewhere that parents are patterns. As in psychological patterns that one must struggle with and ultimately overcome. Such crap. Psychology is such crap.' – Meg

Kavitha Rao is having a spa day with her sisters and is in extremely good spirits for reasons that have nothing to do with oil massages and chocolate pedicures. Her sisters know this because this is the first time she's even setting foot in a spa. After years of trying to persuade her to give herself permission to enjoy some of life's small pleasures and being met with the same display of shock and disbelief at their willingness to spend four thousand rupees on a massage, they are convinced that something else is cooking in Kavitha's life. But what could it be? Vinitha, the younger and more curious of the two, decides to peel off her eye mask in the middle of her facial, pull the partition between her and Kavitha's side of the room, and take a sly peek. It turns out to be totally worth it too since Kavitha seems to be poring over a stack of bridal magazines with great enthusiasm while a frustrated masseuse instructs her to relax.

'Shh…asking me to relax is not relaxing,' she snaps at the masseuse. 'Now, do what you have to do without interrupting my reading.'

Vinitha's eyes widen like she has just stumbled upon a juicy family secret and is off to report it to Anita who is a touch calmer (perhaps something to do with the fact that her parents removed the 'h' in her name?). 'So, what do you think this means?' Anita wants to know.

'I don't know – what if that wastrel husband of hers has made a comeback? Or *oooh*...what if she's met someone?' Vinitha loves a good romance.

'You got all that from the bridal magazine, *aah*?' Anita says.

'What else can explain the sudden switch to this happy, bridal-magazine reading, spa-going Kavitha?' Vinitha has seen this sort of mid-life transformations among suburban wives in the US. She's quite sure her theory is very close to the truth.

'Her mood is odd only...'Anita admits.

'I know what to do! We should follow her. See if there's a man in the picture!' Vinitha says.

'You are missing your US life, *aah*?' Anita is carrying forward the family tradition of ending every question with an 'aah'.

Kavitha walks in, interrupting their plans. 'So, I couldn't help but overhear...'

Vinitha looks worried like a school child caught in the act of some petty mischief. 'We were just...' she stutters and looks helplessly at Anita, the eldest of the siblings, though Kavitha is the most feared.

'Forgive me for spoiling your reality show but the reason I'm in a great mood is because... Meg might get married soon!' she squeals in delight, making the second part of her sentence barely audible.

'Oh, she's marrying that singer boy, *aah*?' Anita says unimpressed.

'He's a handsome boy,' Neel still has Vinitha's vote at least.

'*Chee, chee*...no!' Kavitha makes no attempt to hide her disapproval and general revulsion of artist types. 'He's an architect!' She grins. 'Running his own business in Bangalore!'

'Oh wowwww!' both siblings are suitably impressed and Kavitha finally feels vindicated. Even Anita's daughters – though they never shamed the family by seeking out their own partners – hadn't done half as well for themselves.

'How did she meet him?' Vinitha is more interested in the romance of it all.

'I picked him out for her on a Tamil matrimonial site' Kavitha is even more pleased with herself. 'He's half Malayali though,' she says apologetically. 'But it's okay. I've Skyped with him and I love him. You will too!'

The rest of the day goes in oohs, aahs and a celebratory lunch. As far as these ladies are concerned, Meg is as good as engaged and wedding ideas are flowing. If Kavitha was more emotionally evolved, she'd know that talking about Meg's partner was really about her repairing and reviving her lost bond with her sisters since her own world-famous elopement and, more importantly, it was about proving herself to them – that despite everything, she had managed to raise her daughter right. That in the end, her daughter would be the one upholding the family tradition of marrying a 'decent, well-educated man in a respectable profession'. But luckily for Kavitha, she isn't burdened by any inherent drive for introspection or personal growth.

~

Meanwhile, our heroine and alleged bride-to-be is in at least two kinds of moral conflicts. One: her party planning is going horribly wrong and the band – Three Blind Mice, who were supposed to be the centrepiece of the event – has cancelled on her at the last minute, making her wonder if it would be *outrageously* horrible of her to ask for Neel's help after having rejected him (again) just days ago or you know, just horrible.

Two: Neel's confession of love and more importantly, the dramatic change to back it up this time, has really affected Meg, and she needs time to clear her head. Rajeev showing up at this time can't be a good thing, but how horrible would it make her if she bought time with Rajeev and postponed their meeting, citing the launch party as a reason when the real reason is that she might be considering her ex's offer – outrageously horrible or just horrible? And it is while she's pondering these matters in her heart and driving home from work that her mother calls and puts her on speaker for her beloved long-lost aunts to congratulate her on the 'very good catch'.

New entry in Meg's Filofax:

- *Call caterer and confirm menu*
- *Get the lights guy's contact from Tania*
- *Check with Rajeev if trip postponement is possible*
- *Postpone moral conflict until after the party*

28

'Uranus transits are ultimately about shaking you awake and setting you off on a new path so maybe there's hope after all.' – Tania

'What were you thinking?' Meg yells into the phone once she knows her mother is back in the privacy of her own apartment. She's outraged at her mother for doing something so unlike herself and blurt out the news about Rajeev to her sisters of all people. Especially since she had promised to not put any pressure on Meg about this from the start.

'I know, I know, I'll fix it…it's just…they basically did an *Inception* on me!' Kavitha says. 'Tapped right into my thought process and got all the info out.'

'*Inception*? As in the movie? Really, Mom?'

'But see, we're having our real first fight as mothers and daughters are supposed to!' Kavitha half-means it.

'Just fix it and do it right away. I don't want anyone thinking I'm getting married!' Meg grunts.

'I'm on it!' Kavitha says. 'But everything is okay, no? You haven't changed your mind about Rajeev or something? I mean, of course you can if you want to, but you'll tell me, no…?'

Meg feels the pressure mounting. She has enough on her plate with Neel hovering on the scene again. She really can't have her mother emotionally blackmailing her right now. 'God, Mom. Yes. Now please fix it.'

'Yes what? Meaning yes, you've changed your mind about Rajeev?' The panic in Kavitha's voice is beyond her capacity to mask.

'Meaning yes, I will tell you if I've changed my mind about Rajeev. God.'

'Okay, okay. Don't get mad.'

Meg sighs as she hangs up, makes herself comfortable on the floor and buries her face in her hands. She wishes she could talk to Tania about this, but Tania is doing everything she can to stay emotionally afloat. At times like these, Meg likes to play a mental game called 'Whose Crisis Would I Rather Have Right Now?' It involves comparing her problems with those of others close to her so that she can comfort herself with the thought that everyone is suffering in some way and that the known devil is always better. It's a pessimist's paradise. Except this time, she finds that she'd rather be in Tania's shoes than her own.

See, Meg is an expert at dealing with betrayal since she has great faith in the average human's capacity to let her down in monumental ways and is, therefore, prepared for this contingency. Making a choice between two people she doesn't want to hurt though is a whole other thing. It presents an emotional conflict and Meg hates those. She'd rather be presented with a verdict so that she can decide if she wants it or toss it out the window. But this? This decision isn't just about her. It's about Neel. About Rajeev. About her mother (and now her mother's sisters) and her relationship with her mother. But more importantly, this is about the Goal. She can't imagine making a decision that would upset everything at once, and yet her heartstrings have been well and truly yanked since her encounter with Neel 2.0.

~

Meanwhile in the low-budget romcom that is Tania's life these days, Ryan is done following her around like a puppy, sending 'rescue me' vibes. He seems happier and just so… unafraid. Tania has to admit she's at least curious about the urgent and important matter that he wants to share with her. She's arranged a secret but totally non-shady rendezvous with Ryan today to hear him out once and for all before taking off for Kodaikanal. They are to arrive separately at Ten Downing Street – the pub that Tania and her friends used to frequent a decade ago but haven't set foot in in years. Tania used to love their lunch menu at one point but her reason for picking the place had less to do with the food and everything to do with not running into anyone she knows.

'Day drinker, huh?' Ryan says as he enters the pub..

'Thanks to you,' Tania says dryly, and Ryan smiles like he knows something she doesn't.

'Look. I'm not here to chit-chat. Please just tell me whatever it is that can't wait and I'll be on my way.'

'And leave me to finish my drink alone? Savage.'

It makes Tania furious that he's taking this so lightly and worse, trying to be charming. 'Figured you'd be used to it by now.' Now she's really on a roll and thankfully, Ryan gets it and decides to get straight to the point.

'I'm sorry,' he says. 'I don't know where to begin and I know I don't deserve your forgiveness but…'

'That's right, you don't.'

Ryan takes a deep breath. 'Right. So Shruti and I are not what you think.'

Tania raises an eyebrow but holds herself back from sarcasm.

'We were very young when we got together, and I realized over time that she wasn't in this for her. Or me. It was just about defying her sister. They have a long history and I don't want to get into all that. You could say that Shruti and I have been there for each other through our respective family struggles. But more like friends than partners. We don't...' he searches for the words. 'It's like our relationship always lacked...'

'Passion?' Tania says and Ryan nods.

'Yeah. Passion. And anything other than friendship.'

Tania is now listening without the snarky commentary in her head.

'And I know it sounds absurd, but I suppose I just got used to it. I accepted it. Marrying me would've been the ultimate "fuck you" to her sister. And she really needed it. And like I said, it's absurd but I tend to get very confused when loyalties are in the mix. And we've always been loyal to each other. But it's not love, Tania.'

'So...?' Tania is trying to see the emergency of it all. Why did he have to share this?

'So – and this is where you come in – you reminded me what being in love is supposed to feel like. And I was a coward. I'm so sorry for putting you through this. But I'll always be grateful to you for showing me this.'

Tania manages a smile but is troubled by where this story is headed. 'So, you guys...'

'Shruti and I broke up. After a long heart-to-heart. But we're both sure that it's the right decision. Now I know that this affects you and not in a good way. But I thought I at least owe it to you this time to tell you first.'

Tania can't think of anything to say. Her thoughts reel from Meera to Aditi to being back in a financial rut to their business to Aditi again. But there is also a shred of relief in the mix. She'd no longer have to plan the wedding of the person she's in love with. And it isn't her fault. Well, not exactly. She can always do everything she can to help Aditi, but it doesn't have to be this! The more she thinks about this, the lighter she feels. 'Thank you,' she says. 'Thanks for telling me first.'

He smiles.

'What's the plan now?'

'The plan is to keep apologizing and making it up to you until you completely forgive me. Then, I'll hopefully take you out on a real date.'

Tania senses a flutter inside her chest and judges herself for it. She really does need to work on being a little more pricey. 'All I know is that I have a ton of things to process right now and that I need to inform Aditi about this at the earliest.'

'Of course,' Ryan says. 'Take your time.'

'I'll talk to you soon,' she smiles as they say goodbye.

Wow, Uranus is really living up to its name as the wildcard of astrology.

29

'The thing is, we've always assumed that the answer to Duran Duran's question – who do you need, who do you love, when you come undone – is a person. Maybe it's not a who. Maybe it's a what. Maybe it's Nutella. If we had only known sooner, we could've spared ourselves this mad longing for human connection.' – Meg

Meg's week has gone from dramatic to *Grey's Anatomy*. Thankfully, nobody has died. Yet. Here's a verbal trailer:

- Rajeev has refused to reschedule his trip because he can't wait to see her a minute longer and besides, it would be fun to watch her in action at the launch that he's heard so much about. The truth though – and this is the side that Meg hasn't seen yet – Rajeev is impossibly Arian and cannot let go of an opportunity to have his way, no matter what.
- The launch event is falling apart on a daily basis, and Meg still hasn't found a suitable replacement for the band. Or worked up the courage to call Neel and ask for help.
- And then there is Neel himself. What is she supposed to do with his confession?
- She's not thinking about her mother and the cardiac arrest she'll suffer if she were told at this stage that it wasn't going

to work out with Rajeev and that she hadn't one-upped her sisters after all.

- In all the chaos, Meg has completely handed over charge of their regular client work to her capable team (unofficially, of course) and they seem to have let her down in ways that might only be seen in a sitcom. Long story short, one of their interns was left unsupervised on one of their client's (a prestigious pre-school) social media pages, and accidentally posted something from another client (condom brand). Hiten has, of course, placed the blame squarely on Meg's shoulders and has even managed to convince the entire office of Meg's 'unstable condition these days'. In his defence, Meg has been constantly fluctuating between euphoric moods and bouts of stress-induced yelling, all culminating in this mega social media fiasco that led to the client cancelling their contract with the agency. Tania calls this 'a classic Mercury retrograde disaster'.
- Hiten has made it quite clear to Meg that the launch party is her last chance to redeem herself or else… Well, not in so many words. That's not his style.

If our heroine was being the logical person she claims she is, she'd admit she needs help and that this launch is impossible to pull off. But that's the thing about complexes. They are blind spots. They work like compulsive inner drives that, well, *drive* you to do things you wouldn't otherwise imagine you could. So, no, she isn't going to admit to Hiten, of all people, that she can't do this. In fact, she'd rather risk her place in the company (because that's basically what Hiten implied by his underplayed threat) than admit that she, Meghana Rao, needs help. Also, with so many seams of her life unravelling all at once, you can't really blame her for trying to keep it together by telling herself and everybody else that everything is under control. Because Meg is nothing if not controlled. There is nothing that terrifies her more than chaos, and chaos is exactly what's looming in the background at this point. Ergo, the need to not lose control by being thwarted by events that haven't even taken place.

~

Meanwhile, Tania cannot wait to share her Ryan news with Meg. She has barely seen her all week, and she's determined to stay up and catch up with Meg today when she gets in from work. It doesn't matter how old you are, there are some things you need your special person for. And Meg and Tania have always been each other's person. They just don't quite know it yet. And tonight is a classic example. Except Meg is exhausted from averting chaos for so long and is most likely to project her anxieties and outrage on Tania.

Tania has been picturing Meg's reaction to the news all week. Somehow, it feels like nothing has really happened until she has shared it with Meg. But when Meg's reaction is so far out on the anticlimactic extreme, Tania has no idea what hit her. And the fact that she needs to present her case to her best friend, who is supposed to be on her side by default, drains her joy by the minute.

'I don't understand,' Tania screams as Meg carefully closes the windows and the balcony door so the neighbours don't hear them. 'Why aren't you happy for me?'

'Right, okay. You broke up someone's engagement at a huge personal cost to your partner, who really needs the money right now. You're right, I didn't see it that way before. Congrats!' Meg sits on the sofa, legs stretched, arms crossed, not in the least interested in hearing Tania's 'side of it'.

'Wow,' Tania says. 'For starters, I did nothing to break up the engagement. You know that! And…'

'You didn't lure him into your office and seduce him or even respond to his attempts to see you alone, but you did ignore the fact that you two shared an intense mutual chemistry and you refused to tell your partner about it!'

'What the fuck are you talking about? I told you there was no other way. I couldn't have told Aditi about that. What would that have achieved? Besides…'

'What would that have achieved? I don't know! Maybe there'd still be a wedding! Maybe she would have found someone else to replace you on this particular assignment and that way, you two wouldn't have been in each other's faces all the time and the wedding would still be on?' Meg seems disproportionately agitated.

'The wedding didn't happen because it wasn't meant to be. I did nothing to disrupt it! And even if I did, the relationship should have been strong enough to take that considering they were planning on spending the rest of their lives together!' Tania is matching Meg's decibel levels now.

'Right. Meant to be. How convenient! Just do what you want and blame the universe for the outcome.'

'I am not denying my part in this. I'm saying I was the trigger that got two people out of a potentially disastrous marriage,' Tania tries to speak calmly.

'And who the hell are you to decide that? God? You *do not* get to decide if two people should be together! I know you think you have a knack for these things but really, what do you know? You know nothing!'

Tania follows the five-second rule that she had read in a self-help book a long time ago to calm down and collect her thoughts. 'Meg,' she says softly, 'what is this really about?'

Meg doesn't say anything. Instead, she mumbles an apology and disappears into her room, leaving Tania depleted but stubbornly clinging to her joy. She drinks a whole bottle of water to eliminate the toxins she might have inadvertently breathed in this exchange with Meg, and settles down on the couch with her phone to grin at the ceiling and text Ryan. She had asked for a week's time to process the news and inform Aditi, and Ryan had happily obliged. She has nothing in particular to say but it's December and she's always felt happy in December, besides Ryan's really in love with her, and this joy must be shared. Tomorrow is going to be a stressful day when she'll have to break the news to Aditi. For the next few minutes as she crafts her text to Ryan, her thoughts swirl around Aditi and the impending doom and gloom that will soon surround her. And as is often the case when you're writing a text to one person but the content itself is about another person, Tania ends up sending the text to Aditi. Except, it's a text, not a WhatsApp message (the social-media-and-chat-averse Ryan is not on WhatsApp) and therefore, it cannot be undone.

'Fuck, no!' she yells and quickly checks the time. It's about 2 a.m. She's going to have to wait till morning to explain herself as Aditi is probably deep in REM sleep right about now.

Fuckfuckfuckfuck, she chants as she reads the text again.

I'm sorry if my reaction was underwhelming when we spoke... I suppose I was still processing the news. I just want you to know that I'm glad you're out of it. And I'm glad the wedding is off. And yes, I'm looking forward to seeing more of you too. This whole experience has sucked for me. Watching you with someone else and planning your wedding was not fun. Whew. Glad it's all over. Keep me updated on how Meera takes the news. Meanwhile, I have Aditi to deal with. Night, night.

Tania spends the rest of the night having palpitations. It's just one of those times when your own words frame you in the worst possible light. She thinks about sending another text to undo the previous one, but wisdom warns her that undo texts are the worst texts, and so she refrains and braces herself for Armageddon the next day.

30

'When the going gets tough, the tough sometimes have to call their exes for help, which is a tough decision, and hence they are tough people.' – Meg

The truly fascinating thing about Meg is her ability to be completely unaware of how close she is to a breakdown. When she was a child, and there were no adults around to set boundaries for her or discipline her when she refused to eat or go to bed on time, Meg formed the habit of making to-do lists in order to hold herself accountable. Somehow the lack of parental authority in her life at that age made her feel like she was missing out on a fundamental part of childhood. So, she made long to-do lists every day, and on some days, she'd carry over her tasks to the next. At some point, when the list became too long, she'd get overwhelmed by anxiety and fall asleep on the couch in the middle of the day instead of keeping at her tasks. If she couldn't complete all of them, there was no way she could derive any satisfaction from completing *some* of them. This piece of Meg's childhood is an essential reference point to her current attitude towards the launch party, which can only be summed up as cavalier. She has reached the adult equivalent of an impossible to-do list and has mentally fallen asleep on the couch.

'There's no way I'm calling Neel,' she says out loud to an empty living room.

'You say that like you have a choice,' says the voice in her head. 'Neel is your "Hail Mary" to salvaging this party.'

'Nah, I'm screwed anyway. Hiten won't miss the opportunity to make me look incompetent and what was that? Unstable!'

'Surely you're not going to let Hiten Shroff of all people make you look incompetent,' the voice says. This seems to work on Meg, and she picks up her phone and calls Neel with the urgency of someone who could change her mind in seconds. Luckily for her, Neel answers immediately.

'Meg?' he says.

'Neel...hi.'

'Hey...' There is an understandable expectancy in his voice. This is the first time they're speaking since they bumped into each other and he said all those lovely things and she basically slammed the door in his face. *Crap, crap, crap*. How is she supposed to tell him now that she isn't calling about that but to actually ask if he and his band would come to her rescue and play at their launch at short notice?

'Hey...' she says again and scolds herself for thinking she could pull this off. 'I was just...uhh...I was just calling to check in on you.'

There's a pause at the other end. 'Oh,' he says. 'I'm good, I guess. How are you?'

'I'm good...good. Yeah, I'll go now. I just wanted to see how you were doing after...yeah, I'll go now.'

'Meg?' Neel says in his who-are-you-trying-to-kid voice.

'Yeah?'

'What do you need?'

'What do you mean?' Meg wishes she could sound more

convincing, but it's taking every ounce of strength to not bawl her eyes out right about now. Neel has always been such an excellent source of comfort, and it feels like a special kind of punishment to have him so close and not be able to tell him how her life has been coming apart strand by strand.

'Meghana Rao. I know you enough to know that you don't do check-ins. Especially when you don't have any answers. In fact, you'd rather avoid me right now but if you're calling, then you're in all kinds of trouble. And being the semi-decent human being that I know you are, you can't work up the courage to tell me. So let me give you a temporary free pass to call in a favour after which I will go back to being mad at you for being such a cold and distant bitch.'

Meg lets out a sigh of relief and at this moment, she understands why her emotions are so stubbornly bonded to him. 'It's the launch party…' She proceeds to fill him in on Hiten and Red Dot, the merger, the cold wars, the recent social media debacle and yes, the launch party for which she's desperately lacking a band.

'Wow,' Neel says at the end of it. 'It's like we've swapped places. Suddenly, my life is all put together and…'

'Yeah, check you out! With not just a job but working with a glamorous, world-famous culinary wizard…'

'Oh, and this is a super-secret but I have to tell you – I'm going to be doing a TV show with Sanjay and the shoot begins next week!'

'Wow,' Meg says, 'I'm so proud of you.' She means it. This is much more than what she had initially wanted for him. She just wishes it had come at a better time. Now Neel is in the best place he's ever been – a successful, trendy job, a band that's coming out with an album – he's so close to being a legit celebrity and her life couldn't be more foggy. And she had rejected him purely because *he* lacked direction!

'Thanks,' Neel says. He means it too. Somehow Meg's approval has always meant the world to him.

'So, you're halfway to being a celebrity, and I'm in a soup. Sorry, culinary pun!'

He laughs. 'Well, don't worry about the launch. We'll be there.'

'Are you serious?' Meg feels like the luckiest party planner on the planet.

'Absolutely. We're in town and doing nothing, so why not?'

'Neel…thank you…I don't know how…'

'Shhhh! Like I said, I plan on going back to being very mad at you after this.'

'Thank you.'

'You're welcome.'

'Byc.'

'Bye.'

31

'You can do everything right but if the universe has scheduled a complete fuck-over for you on Tuesday, there's really nothing much you can do about it and that can't be your fault.' – Tania

Tania wakes up at around 8 a.m., having dozed off at some point during the hypothetical arguments and counterarguments she was busy constructing in her head. She is blissfully ignorant of what day it is for half a second till glimpses of the previous night flash before her eyes and she's wide awake. This is the worst kind of morning-after she thinks before checking her phone in a hurry. No calls or texts from Aditi, just an ominous 'read' on iMessage that just hangs there, silently speaking of looming danger. *Maybe she's waiting for me to call and explain*, Tania wonders optimistically. And mistakenly.

She calls Aditi. No answer. Maybe she's just in the shower. Or attending to her recovering husband. Or getting her kid ready for school. Could be anything. No need to panic just yet, she tells herself. Again, optimistically.

Tania spends a whole hour in the shower trying to imagine what her day might be like. When all scenarios end badly, she decides reality might just be better than this, summons the courage to turn off the shower, get, dressed and is ready to hear from Aditi.

'It seems he was already married or something,' she overhears Nandu discussing the most private details of her life with Meenakshi Aunty from her balcony.

'How the fuck could they possibly know?' Tania says to herself and decides it's a pointless question with answers that couldn't be comforting.

She checks her phone again when she's in the cab. Still nothing from Aditi. Resisting the nausea that's quickly building up, she urges herself to breathe in and out. She calls Aditi again. Still no answer. She decides she better text her.

> `We need to talk. Also, that message was a case of bad timing and the wrong choice of words and other cosmic bloopers. I'm sure you're used to my poor texting skills by now, haha.`

She hits send without reading. Immediately, she thinks *Should I have not added that 'haha'?* Afterthoughts. Bloody afterthoughts. *Oh god, now she's going to think I found the whole thing funny. But why did I say 'haha' if I didn't? I was just being ironic. No, I wasn't. I was hoping she'd realize that it was so obvious to me that this was a mistake and so it must be obvious to her too. Oh fuck. I can't wait for this day to end.*

When Tania reaches the office, Aditi is already there. Her face looks drained of colour and more angular today than usual since there's no smile to soften the edges. She stares blankly at Tania as she approaches.

'Hey,' Tania starts slowly and cautiously.

Aditi gestures for her to stop. 'Please don't say anything,' she says. 'I'm running on very little energy these days, and I'd like to not throw it away on you.'

Tania's heart chakra starts to spin like a top. 'Aditi, please. Listen to me. I know what I sent but it's really, really not what it sounded like – I swear!'

'I said I don't want to hear it,' Aditi's tone is searing and while Tania's afraid of it, she's not going to back down until she's been heard. 'So please just pack your things and get the hell out of this office. I'll settle your dues as soon as I can because we're done here.'

Now Tania's heart chakra has taken a break but the solar plexus one – the seat of personal power – is spinning with purpose. 'That's not fair! This is a partnership. You owe me the decency of hearing me out! And this is my office too!' Tania's voice is getting louder by the second, but Aditi seems unmoved, and calm even, making her appear twice as formidable.

'How dare you talk to me about fairness, partnerships and decency after what you've done?'

'I have done nothing,' Tania says feebly, tears streaming down her cheeks. Why is she crying? She's actually angry. Bloody Mars in Cancer always makes her feel so impotent when she really should be exploding with rage. 'Like I said, that message has given you the wrong picture!'

Aditi sighs, walks up to Tania and meets her eyes like a prosecutor who means business. 'So, tell me. Did you or did you not have some kind of personal history with Ryan before you knew him as your client?'

'Yes but –

'Just the answer, please.'

'Yes, I did.'

'When you promised me that you would come through and

make sure this wedding was a success, did you understand what you were saying?'

Tania gulps. 'Yes.'

'Did you or did you not then proceed to hide the crucial fact of your involvement with the groom from me, knowing exactly what was at stake?'

'But I couldn't have told –'

'Did you or did you not?'

'I did.'

'Great. Now, were you or were you not aware that the one thing I do not tolerate in my close relationships is dishonesty?'

Tania closes her eyes but that doesn't stop the embarrassing gush of tears. 'Yes,' her voice is shaky.

Aditi smiles shortly. 'So that's it. We *are* done here.'

And with that, Aditi walks back into her office and gets on with work as usual as if her partnership has not just come crashing down. Tania leaves, all her chakras on strike and her future, blurrier than ever.

And as is the case with people facing curveballs in their lives, Tania too is prone to behaving in ways that she can't quite understand. And while most of us would probably change our hairstyle, binge watch Netflix for a whole month or get a piercing, Tania's way of dealing with her newfound chaos is heading straight to the Blue Cross and adopting a…goat (only because everyone wants to rescue puppies and kittens, and poor white-as-snow Elsa the goat kid has no takers and that's just wrong).

32

'When neck-deep in a crisis, I find it helpful to remind myself that this is the part in a Bollywood movie that would disappear in a bad montage and a sad song by the end of which, the hero will somehow know what to do.' – Tania

Meg's journal entry from the night before the launch party:

- *My band cancelled last minute and had to be replaced with my ex's band.*
- *The caterers got the wrong order (we're now getting first-birthday themed food) and I can't cancel 'cause no one's going to be able to take an order this late anyway*
- *The lights' guy tells me now that he lost most of his stuff in a freak accident last week, and all he's now left with are something resembling fairy lights and a ton of white lights.*
- *My colleagues don't believe me. They think I'm setting it all up for a big surprise. Tania says, 'But of course, baby. Who throws a party during Mercury Retrograde?'*
- *And the icing on the cake: Rajeev Menon is in town and since I'm going to be at the party, he has very kindly agreed to meet me there. Now, I don't just have to worry about my work life falling apart, I actually have to look good while it does. So, I've decided to turn the party into a parody. The party that mocks parties. At this point, I don't have much of a choice given that all I have are fairy lights, baby-themed food and an amateur band (God bless Neel!). In*

fact, I'm going to hire a guy to stand in the middle of the room with a crowd around him, wearing a T-shirt that says 'Life.' You know? Life of the Party. Maybe once everyone's sufficiently inebriated, we'll have Life walking around the room, distributing lemons. When Hiten comes after me, I'll just tell him he didn't get my highbrow comedy and quit before he fires me.

It's the morning after the wildly jinxed launch party and our heroine is about to wake up to a little more than a headache and embarrassment over party mishaps. She is about to wake up to 'the morning after the night' she will need to work on with a therapist for a good long time.

See, Meg has never found hook-ups appealing despite her many sincere efforts at embracing promiscuity. Mostly because it involved waking up to a tequila hangover (the aforementioned sincere effort could only be set in motion by tequila) and going on a humiliating hunt for her underwear through a stranger's bedroom floor. What's worse, it was always followed by a meltdown on her own bathroom floor, an experience she chalked down to Catholic guilt acquired from Catholic school. All in all, she reckoned, there was nothing in it for her except shame, misery and a pounding head. She has since observed abstinence while single and restricted herself to one partner when not – the current phase being the abstinence phase.

You can imagine the regret and self-loathing mingled with nausea Meg experiences as she wakes up this morning in a strange apartment. 'Nonononono' the familiar chant begins in her head as she tries to extricate herself from under the duvet without waking up whoever lies behind her. But surprise, surprise, Meghana Rao is fully clothed. In the same clothes she was in last night. Hmm, she considers this with surprise and relief and holds her head with both hands, hoping to shake out all the missing pieces of the night before. She's still not ready to turn around for fear of whom she might find there. It doesn't matter that her clothes are in place, it's still a strange apartment, and there are plenty of things one can do with one's clothes on that would upset Meg just as much as a full-blown hook-up.

Please don't be Hiten! Please don't be Hiten! Please don't be Hiten.

'Hey, you're up.' A familiar voice. Meg turns around very slowly so as to not frighten away the air of disbelief she has going on. Neel. It's Neel in all his sharp jawline and bedhead glory.

'Neel,' she says, trying to hide the surprise in her tone. 'Oh, hey. Morning!'

He's been watching her for a while, and he hasn't missed that she's got her 'still processing' face on. He smiles at her attempt at breeziness. 'You don't remember a thing and you're freaking out, aren't you?'

'Oh god! Yes! Tell me everything!' She doesn't care that she's woken up with Neel. She's relieved she hasn't hooked up with a stranger and most of all, that she doesn't have to pretend to be breezy about it.

Neel chuckles, yawns and stretches all at once, knowing exactly what it's going to do to Meg to be kept waiting. 'Let's go back to sleep. I'll tell you when we're up.' He rolls over and buries his face under a pillow.

'No!' Meg yanks the pillow away, while summoning her last smidgen of self-restraint to not let her eyes linger on his shoulders. Neel had always been proud of his, iron-pumping arms but it is the shoulders that made Meg want to indulge in shockingly un-Meg-like acts. 'Get up! You're telling me now!' She smacks him with the pillow and in one ju-jitsu-y manoeuvre, he pins her to the bed, and while being pinned under those magnificent shoulders, Meg chooses not to notice when self-restraint makes a quiet, polite exit.

~

Fuckfuckfuckfuck. 'I manage to keep my clothes on through the worst night of my life and a drunken stupor to boot but now, in the morning, I decide to have casual sex?' Meg is having one of her famous post-coital talks with herself and Neel is enjoying it.

'Well, it doesn't have to be casual.'

'Don't. I'm thinking.'

'Right,' he makes his way into the shower as Meg tries to make sense of herself and the last half hour.

'This has never happened before! I have never hooked up casually when sober!' By now she's speaking too loudly for it to qualify as a conversation with herself.

'Uhh, I'm flattered?' Neel calls out from the shower. 'You want to go grab breakfast?'

'You want to go stay locked up in the past where you belong?' She immediately regrets saying it. Neel may have a high level of tolerance for her crazy, but he isn't built for coldness and her tendency to be abrasive without warning. And he doesn't deserve this. 'I'm sorry, I'm just mad at myself. This isn't about you. I'm sorry,' she mumbles but Neel is already behind her, squishing her with long, wet arms.

'It's fine. You're going to be fine. We're going to be fine.'

For a second, she wants to press pause. This feels good and safe and she isn't quite sure, but she suspects it feels 'right'. But Meg being Meg has to analyse and validate the feeling before giving in to it. Neel seems to instinctively understand her need to do this and releases her gently and begins to get dressed.

'There's no we. We broke up!' Meg panics a minute too late.

'I know. I meant we, as individuals, are going to be fine with our separate lives.' He really is a patient guy.

Meg is immediately more at ease and demands that he bring her up to speed on the previous night.

~

An hour later, Meg is in her own living room, relieved to see Tania there. She really needs her sounding board right now. If everything that Neel had said about last night was, in fact, true and not a cruel practical joke, she really needs to get it out of her system and into Tania's right about now.

'All right, I'm going to tell you something – actually, a ton of things – and I need you to not react.' Meg is so consumed by her drama at the moment that she hasn't noticed the completely spaced out expression on Tania's face.

'Bullet points of the party last night:

- Nobody got the parody. It was just a really bad party.
- Rajeev Menon insisted on picking me up by cab and taking me to the party because he wanted to treat me "like a lady all evening". I was so preoccupied with the party, I didn't pay attention to the red flag. Now that I think about it, he has said things like that before. But I'm not sure – I forget the context now.
- Radioactive Chutney was the only saving grace but not enough, apparently. Yes, that's right, Neel and Rajeev at the same party. Thankfully, that introduction didn't happen as I didn't have any time for Rajeev and worse, didn't even

have the time to even realize that or feel bad about it. At one point, I noticed that he looked miffed and I tried to talk to him, but I was interrupted.

- Hiten was hopping mad and said insulting things to my face for a change.
- The argument got nasty, I felt humiliated and therefore, I parked myself at the bar. By this time, Rajeev was nowhere to be seen. I assumed he had left but really couldn't care given everything else.
- At one point, I declared a food fight, and Hiten was basically my dartboard.
- Along the way, Rajeev who had mysteriously vanished, happened to return just in time to see Neel carrying me – slurring, kicking heels and all – to his car.
- I ended up at Neel's place, a hot mess and begged him to "do something stupid with me". (I suspect he embellished this part.)
- He tucked me in bed, clothes and residual dignity intact.
- I woke up and did something stupid with him – eyes wide open and fully sober.

Soooo, this means:

- I may not have a job.
- The Neel episode felt surprisingly good but that's not me, that's oxytocin speaking.
- I'm the unforgettable date from hell in Rajeev's life. In his romcom, I will be that wild child he once went on a date with. Did you hear that? Wild child! Me! I find this oddly satisfying – that I'm the wild child in someone's story.
- He did seem like a nice guy though, so if there was potential, I totally made sure I blew it.'

Tania is still silent. 'Okay, I know I asked you not to react but please say something now.' Still nothing. 'Is that...a goat...in our apartment?' Meg is finally registering things around her and the fact that while Tania seems to be physically present there is really no one in there. 'Tan...? What's going on?

'Aditi threw me out of our business. I sent her the text I was supposed to send Ryan. She got the whole thing wrong and won't listen to me.' She speaks with the deadpan expression of someone who has exhausted herself from crying and overthinking.

'Oh my god!' Meg goes over to the couch and settles herself next to Tania, pulling her into a hug. 'You're going to get through this. We're both going to.' Of course, she has no idea *how* since she hasn't the faintest clue what to expect when she heads to work the next day or how she's supposed to break the news about Rajeev to her mother or what exactly might be the next steps with Neel and most importantly, if there should be a next step. But even with all this, Meg is quietly grateful that she hasn't reached the 'adopt-a-goat' stage of the breakdown yet.

33

'Why do they say "Don't be a quitter" like it's a bad thing? Knowing when to quit is a sign of self-respect. I'm just being emotionally healthy – or something.' – Meg

It's the Monday after the Monday after the party, and Meg steadies herself as she makes her way to the sixth floor of the building where the Red Dot W&P office is. After the humiliating party experience and the showdown with Hiten in full view, Meg had thought a week's break might be good to clear her head and surprisingly, so did Hiten. But it now feels a lot like the first day of school. Except instead of butterflies, it feels like there might be tiny rodents in there, nibbling away at her intestines. She has thought it all through – the mandatory HR rounds that will happen about the showdown, the following meltdown and, not to mention, the series of disasters that ensured their launch was a joke. It was scOOPS' – the website that covers advertising industry news – cover story for the month. All things considered, Meg is quite surprised that the whole fiasco didn't end with her getting fired on multiple counts, especially insubordination. If a couple of HR rounds is what it would take to make amends, she is more than prepared for it. Except, nothing is ever so straight and simple with Hiten.

When Meg enters the office, it's empty and pitch dark. She steps outside, checks if she's got off on the right floor just to be sure. But the Red Dot W&P board is right there in red and purple. She steps in again tentatively and gropes her way to the light switch being careful not to trip over her own feet. She turns it on and there's her recurring nightmares: a room full of cheery people yelling 'Surprise!' Nothing makes Meg more anxious and queasy than happy things she can't see coming. It's just her belief that good things call for notice 'because the anticipation is the best part'. And surprises – whether a sudden weekend getaway or a good old-fashioned birthday surprise – steal that from you. They also cheat you out of necessary preparation such as waxed legs. But back to Red Dot W&P.

Meg is visibly surprised, though 'weirded out' is the term she's going with in her head, and everyone is pleased. It's not her birthday and she can't think of any good reason why people might be celebrating her return. But here they are – sprinkling confetti, distributing cake and pizza – and Meg can't make any sense of it. Maybe they really are that happy to have her back. Maybe they realize what a slimy, underhanded snake Hiten is and missed her being in charge. But Hiten is right there. He's beaming. Like he was the one who orchestrated the whole thing. But why would he? She was expecting him to give her a hard time or at the very least, keep her out of important projects, not celebrate. Something isn't adding up.

'Meg, how are you holding up, sweetie?' the sweet grandma of an admin lady enquires just as Meg tries to give Hiten the benefit of the doubt and grabs a slice of pizza.

'Oh, I'm good, Vaishnavi,' Meg says.

Vaishnavi places a comforting hand on her arm. 'Good, good. We're all here for you. Remember that.' As Meg nods vaguely and continues to focus on her pizza, Nitin and gang approach her somewhat cautiously.

'All good?' Nitin asks.

'Yeah,' Meg says.

'Good, good,' they all say in unison with an air of nervousness.

'Guys! What's going on? Why is everyone tip-toeing around me? I mean I get that I lost it at the party, but you guys have seen me lose it before.' Meg is beginning to get seriously unnerved by all the attention and is hoping one of her perhaps formerly close colleagues might offer an explanation, but all she gets is more comfort, reassurances that everything is fine, and well-meaning advice to relax and try meditation. She spends the rest of the day trying to get an audience with the mighty Hiten, but he's mysteriously caught up in meetings. Things finally come to a head at 4 p.m. when there's a special talk on mental health awareness and how there is no shame in asking for help. This might have gone unnoticed considering they did often have talks on various issues except that this time, the entire office seemed to be sending her support and reassurance via sustained eye contact every time her eyes accidentally meet theirs.

'That's it!' Meg mutters to herself as she leaves the room and barges into Hiten's office. Hiten pretends to be on an important call but Meg isn't having any of it.

'What the fuck, Hiten?' Meg may be a small person but as she stands there, in front of her boss, hands on her hips, feet slightly apart and nostrils flared in rage, she is fierce. Hiten immediately gets off the call on cue.

'Meg, why don't you have a seat! Sorry, I've been busy…'

'Why does everyone think I'm insane?' Meg asks, still standing.

'Now, now, that's not quite the word I'd use. And come on, didn't you learn anything from today's talk? There is no shame in accepting help when you're feeling a little...you know... unstable!'

And suddenly, it all adds up. This is Hiten's story to salvage the launch disaster and humiliating coverage on various industry news portals: the employee who had handled the party had had mental health issues that no one was aware of. But instead of sacking her for the disaster that has cost the company so much, the new management has decided to come together as a family and be supportive. This way, he not only explained away the disaster, he managed to come across as progressive, socially aware and as someone who places a very high premium on empathy. *Wow,* she thinks as she pieces the puzzle together. *I must hand it to him for possessing such a brilliantly scheming, diabolical mind.*

'Fuck you, Hiten,' she says. 'You're an idiot if you think I'm going down without a fight.

'Meg, you're overreacting.'

'You have spread rumours about my emotional instability to an entire industry and I'm overreacting?'

'Anyone who's watched the video footage from that evening would concur that it was much more than a display of emotional instability,' Hiten says calmly as Meg's eyes smoulder with rage. 'But we're willing to go past all that for someone who has contributed so many years to the company. We're offering you a fresh start but you're going to have to work with us here, Meg.'

'Screw you.' Meg makes her way out, grabs her things and leaves the office without saying goodbye to her old friends who now think she's bipolar, thanks to the rumours Hiten has so carefully seeded. She pauses and takes one last glance at the place that has been home for so many years, during her worst emotional fallouts, her reason for getting out of bed in the morning. Meg has always been aware of her capacity to burn bridges in a second if the situation called for it, but this was the one place she had never imagined leaving so unceremoniously. She had planned on moving away only when she was ready to start her own agency, leaving behind colleagues who couldn't be consoled and shoes no one could fill. In this fantasy, STD flies down to Chennai just to ensure that she gets the best damn send-off in the history of Red Dot.

Now, not only has STD mentally checked out since the merger (though it's been downhill since his divorce), the entire industry will now remember her as the emotionally unstable woman who used to work at Red Dot. Hot tears line the inside of her eyelids, but Meg is determined not to break down here. After all, if she's being really honest with herself, this place stopped challenging her a while ago. She had become complacent and bored, and she was really only in it for the stability she couldn't bear to part with. Maybe Tania was right. 'Sometimes when going through difficult astrological transits, it can feel like the universe is snatching away something out of your hands, but that's only the subjective experience – you're holding on to something you've really outgrown but don't have the eyes to see it just yet.' Yes, that's it, she concedes.

'Goodbye, Red Dot,' she whispers, holding back the tears that are demanding to be let out now. 'We had a good run.'

34

'If you love something or think you could love it, vet it thoroughly and do not let emotions get in the way while carrying out intensive background checks.' – Meg

It has been a week since life blew up in her face, and Meg is going about her day with the smug assumption that the proverbial shit has hit the fan and she's still, being the stoic person that she is, keeping it together. She doesn't know yet that shit has only been warming up so far and that by the time it's done with her, she'll begin to question everything she's believed about herself and the world, and that it will be the true turning point of her adult life. But seeing Tania in this miserable, faithless state (she's completely disenchanted with spirituality, New Age ideas, astrology and faith itself, and has even made a statement by throwing out her closet full of tarot and oracle cards) is encouragement enough for Meg to hold herself back from spiralling. Besides, there are perks to unemployed living: sleep, more sleep, Netflix (god, just how many good shows are they making these days?) and not having to feel responsible for everything. In fact, everything is good except for the fact that one key person in her life has no clue about recent events: job, Rajeev, Neel. And Meg is not looking forward to breaking the news to her.

'You can't avoid telling your mom forever, you know,' Tania says, fondly stroking Elsa the goat as she bleats approvingly.

'Says the crazy goat lady who hasn't breathed a word about her boy drama to her own mother, let alone how the boy drama led to her losing her job, friend and general reputation?'

'FYI, I'm headed to Kodai this weekend and am staying there indefinitely – I'll fill her in then,' Tania says, and Meg looks up, shocked and feeling left out. It was easier not dealing with her mother when she knew that Tania, who was pretty much in the same boat, wasn't dealing with hers.

'Excellent. Now I'm the only one who has mother drama. Speaking of, she hasn't called me since the day before yesterday, which is not ominous at all.'

Tania chuckles in spite of herself. 'Don't read into it. Just call her. She might be mad for a while, but I'm sure she'll understand. You guys have a thing now.'

'Yeah, see that's the problem. This *thing*. I was quite happy without the thing. I didn't have to explain myself or my actions to anyone. Now I don't just have to deal with my own mess, I have to worry about how she'll take it and how my decisions affect her!'

'You get that that's what it means to have a relationship with another person, right?'

'Shut up,' Meg grunts, and Tania chuckles.

'So, you're really done with the planets and tarot and the woo-woo-there-is-a-meaning-to-every-coincidence thing huh?'

'I don't know,' Tania says. 'I don't know what I believe in anymore. I thought I was doing everything right considering my options – and god knows my intentions were pure, and yet it still blew up in my face…'

'Yeah,' Meg says in solidarity. She's pretty disenchanted with her own beliefs. She did everything by the book too and yet despite all her hard work and self-restraint, her emotions or whatever that compulsive inner force was, tripped her up again. 'And Ryan?'

'I haven't taken his calls and he hasn't tried to call since last week. I just…I can't, right now. It's just all messed up and the timing is all kinds of off. I can't.'

'Yeah.'

~

'Mom, I know you're mad that I didn't let you meet Rajeev, but that just might be a good thing 'cause I have something important to tell you, and it would help if you stopped ignoring my calls and picked up the phone.' Meg leaves a voice message for her mother who, as it turns out, has been ignoring her instead of the other way around for the last three days and Meg had been too busy stewing in too-much-Netflix-induced self-loathing to notice.

'God,' Meg mutters out loud, 'why do I always have to take care of other people when I'm the one with the problems?' She realizes there's no one else in the room, not even Elsa, whom Tania has taken for a walk (with leash, collar and everything) and decides to go back to Netflix. But just as she's all settled in in bed, pizza on a plate (she may be losing her mind but she's still Meg and she'd never eat pizza out of the box) and Netflix opened on her laptop, there's an email – yes, an email – from her mother.

'More and more ominous,' Meg says under her breath as she proceeds to open it.

'The time for calling and explaining is over,' is all the email says and comes with pictures of the launch party attached, including a video recording of a very inebriated Meg embarrassing herself, fighting with her boss and – icing on the cake – being carried by Neel into his car.

'WHAT THE...HOW...WHAT...'

After a whole afternoon of processing the email with Tania, Meg decides to investigate the situation some more on Tania's suggestion, and she hears from the horse's mouth that she got what she deserved and that her mother needed to know what a 'lying, filthy whore' her daughter was. The horse in question being Rajeev Menon, the well-educated, well-travelled architect groom, of course. And that's not all. Rajeev, with the fiery pride and hidden vengeful streak, had to forward said 'evidence' to her aunts as well, whom he easily tracked on Facebook.

This is Meg's first experience with someone who might be an actual psych case and for the first time in her life, she's feeling terrified and unsafe. But most of all, heartbroken that it only took one email for her newfound relationship with her mother to come tumbling down like a house of cards. She has always assumed these things happened to naïve women who 'don't know better' or were simply underequipped when it came to taking care of themselves. But now that she's wrapped up in a blanket with Tania making her tea, trying to make the trembling stop, she's ready to apologize to every woman she may have been condescending towards in the past.

'Shhhh,' Tania holds her tight. 'I say thank god this happened. You dodged a bullet, Meg. Imagine if things had gone well! You could have started a relationship...you could have married him!'

'It's not that,' Meg says, not even trying to hold back the tears anymore. 'It should be my mum making me tea right now, because I'm sure as hell that yours would!'

Tania's heart hurts at the sight of Meg showing so much vulnerability, and she is quietly thankful for her expert coddling skills.

35

'Soulmates don't come by every day. There's a lot I don't know but this, I know.' – Tania

It's been nine days since the showdown (more like let-down) with Aditi, and Tania is beginning to feel the rage she had so masterfully repressed all this time. For starters, how dare Aditi throw her out of the company? Like it was hers alone to begin with. Sure, the space was hers, but what about all the rest of it? And what's up with such unforgiving black-and-white judgement? She hadn't even wanted Meera as a client to begin with. And then to be abandoned and forced to deal with the nine headed serpentine monster all by herself because she – Aditi – needed this wedding and the money and what not. And Tania had handled this conflict so graciously, choosing to bear the burden of responsibility all on her own, considerately keeping her partner out of it because she had enough on her plate, and what does she get? Judgement, and accusations of lies and betrayal. Like her hard work and stoic endurance of this horrible emotional conflict didn't count at all. Like nothing she ever did mattered because in one unguarded moment, she was human! Sure, in a perfect world, she would have managed to handle the conflict and keep her partner in the loop about her involvement with Ryan without burdening her with the consequences of such a confession. But the world isn't perfect, and neither is she.

Tania decides to jump out of bed and jog it off before the unchannelled rage decides to explode at an untimely moment. 'Please don't let me run into Ryan,' she whispers as she gets on the road. It's been 10 days since she's been going for her morning runs and though it's 6.50 a.m., past Virus' walk time, she's worried it might happen. She'd run into him and though she'd want to run past him, Virus would make it impossible. Since she's come to love that dog like her own, she wouldn't be able to resist cuddling him. And Ryan would pick that moment to have the talk he's been trying to have since the disaster, given she's been avoiding his calls. She was not looking forward to that, considering all the rage waiting to erupt. She just might say the wrong thing and ruin this forever. Not that there is much hope right now, but she'd still not like to be the one to burn the bridge.

'Tania...thank god...have you seen him... was it you...is that why he took off?' Speak of the devil and here he comes, panting and seeking help.

'Ryan... What happened? What's going on? Where's Virus?'

Ryan tries to take a breath. 'I was walking him, and he's been all right all this time but today, for some reason, he was cranky, and he just took off...the leash just snapped!'

'Took off? What do you mean he just took off? Where could he go? Ryan...'

'I couldn't keep up with him and I got blocked by traffic and...god knows... He wouldn't make it through traffic.' Ryan's voice goes from pleading to breaking. Tania takes a moment to pull herself together and put away all frightening thoughts of Virus wading his way through traffic before calling all the animal rescue people she knows. 'Yeah, golden retriever male, he's about eight or nine months old, very energetic, wears a red collar and responds to Virus.' Tania makes call after panicked call. 'Come on, we should get going too,' she tells Ryan and they start to run in the direction Ryan last saw him jet off.

'I just don't understand...' Ryan is still in a state of shock. 'Why would he run away like that?'

'Could've been anything! A cat, another dog...was he chasing something?'

'I don't know,' Ryan says. 'I was on the phone. I really shouldn't have been on the phone!'

Tania reaches out and pats his back. 'This isn't your fault,' she says. It's the first time they're making eye contact since, well, everything. 'You're a good dad, Ryan.'

Ryan makes a deliberate effort to hold it together. 'I have to find him.'

'And we will. He couldn't have gone very far, and my rescue buddies are great at what they do. They're all on it. You're lucky they all live a stone's throw away. Just try to have faith and be patient,' she says in spite of herself. 'We're going to find him. The universe can't be that cruel either.'

After a couple of hours of relentless searching through every neighbourhood street, they decide to sit by the tea shop at the corner of the street Ryan lives on and wait for news. It's a spot Virus is familiar with as well.

'I cannot lose him,' Ryan says. 'This year has taken enough from me.'

Tania senses the inevitable conversation coming and so she jumps right in. 'Ryan, it's just... really bad timing' she says. 'I've lost everything over this non-relationship relationship. I don't have a job to go back to or even know what I want to do. There's so much I still need to process and figure out. I know it seems like I'm punishing you by being cold and locking you out, but I don't have an answer to give you right now because I don't know what I want or who I am or...what I believe in anymore.'

'I understand,' he says, making eye contact, and apparently, it's gooey-place-in-my-heart eye contact because in that moment, Tania feels fully convinced that this is her soulmate. It's a knowing she can't shake off. But Tania isn't the same person anymore. She's learnt not to trust 'knowing' which isn't built on reality, on a solid foundation, so she chooses not to act on it.

'But once we find Virus, I'm leaving the city,' he says and it's Tania's turn to swallow hard and hold back the fears that come charging in her direction. Fears of losing her soulmate forever. A soulmate she never imagined she'd find.

'Leaving the city...?'

'Yeah, I'm going back to Pune,' he says half-meeting her eyes. 'I'm not yet sure what I'll do but that city has a way of bringing me back to myself...'

The phone rings and they both jump. 'I think I just found your boy,' Tania's friend says, and the unmistakable sound of Virus' disapproving growl in the background confirms it. Ryan and Tania are elated. 'Thank you, thank you, thank you!' Ryan screams into the phone. 'I owe you big time!'

'Ask me where I found him?'

'Where?' Tania and Ryan say in unison.

'He was stalking a shih-tzu and refused to leave their doorstep. Right here on 8th Street. I think maybe your boy is ready for a girlfriend.'

'Wow,' Ryan says, when they're done with the whole ordeal and Virus has come home. 'At least *he* knows how to go after what he wants before it's too late.'

'Ryan…' Tania says. She can't seem to get her words in order. She wants to ask him to stay but is afraid of doing to him what he's done to her – dragging him into uncertainty with her.

'No, it's fine,' he says, kissing her on the forehead. 'It's probably better this way, you know?'

'Probably.'

'For someone who came into my life so recently and in the most random manner, you've stood by me through the breaking up of my engagement, losing and finding my dog and still stayed committed to training the world's worst dog.'

Tania smiles. 'When you put it like that…'

'I'm so glad I ran into you that morning.'

'Ditto,' Tania says and takes off before the floodgates open.

36

'No, I still think gut feelings are all hogwash. But there is merit in testing theories which is what I'm doing.' – Meg

Things Meg's been writing in her journal:

- *I have not yet let go of all the unresolved anger with Rajeev but I'm working on it. It's definitely not worth my time or energy. Not sure if I'm ready to let go of the part of me that got me into that mess though. That would mean NOT taking life into my own hands, and why would I not do that?*
- *To therapy or not to therapy? Hell, I'm the most emotionally stable, reasonable person I know. I do not need therapy!*
- *Okay, but what now? Which piece of my mangled life do I pick up first? And what am I supposed to do with it after? Wait, isn't that the kind of question that qualified therapists are supposed to help you answer?*
- *Perhaps I could go to therapy, but really, it isn't therapy at all. It's more like paying an objective third party to listen to you and offer advice from their unique position as an objective third party.*
- *Yeah, that's it. I don't have to call it therapy if I don't want to and I don't have to tell anyone. Because it's not therapy.*
- *Must stop saying therapy.*

Meg tiptoes out of her bedroom to see what Tania is up to. She really doesn't want Tania to find out about this or she'll make it a bigger deal than necessary. And right now, Meg is kind of wired about the idea, having debated the pros and cons all night. In fact, this is the most workable short-term goal on her agenda now. This is the solution to everything. It will sort out her head and help her achieve clarity so she can move forward again.

The sound of the washing machine indicates it's Tania's laundry day. And laundry day is a sort of sacred ritual for Tania, symbolic of washing away the past. So, she isn't going to be walking into Meg's room anytime soon. Perfect. Meg tiptoes back into her room, locks the door behind her and pulls out the business card that Tania had given her weeks ago. Shyama Nambiar, it says. She calls the hospital for an appointment but can't seem to get through.

'Dammit!' she flings the phone on her bed. This is the beauty of Meg. She may take forever to make up her mind about something she's naturally resistant to, but once she does and things do not go her way, she'll behave like she's been convinced of said thing all her life.

'Good breath in, bad breath out,' Meg orders herself to calm down and tries the hospital again. It finally rings!

'Good morning, Trinity Hospital. How may I help you?' asks a very bored voice that by all indications seemed uninterested in helping out.

'Hi, I'm calling for an appointment with Shyama Nambiar,' Meg says.

'Shyama Ma'am has gone to the US, madam,' the receptionist says dismissively.

'Oh,' Meg feels a sinking sensation in her chest. It's not that there are no other therapists in town but for once in her adult life, she had decided to surprise herself, change strategy and go with her gut feeling. And she had had a feeling about this one. Somehow she had felt that the first place she called would just work out.

'Call after two months, madam, thank you,' the receptionist is about to hang up.

'Uh...hang on! Are there any other therapists at your hospital?' Meg asks hopefully.

'No madam, sorry,' comes the instant response and Meg is officially deflated.

'Thanks,' she says and hangs up. Afraid to return to her day. Another day without a plan. 'So much for going with the gut,' Meg mutters under her breath.

As if on cue, the phone rings. It's the hospital. 'Hello?'

'Madam, calling from Trinity Hospital.'

'Yeah, tell me?'

'Are you okay with a junior psychotherapist?' Meg's heart begins to pick up pace again, but she's not sure she likes the sound of junior.

'Uhh...how junior?'

'Madam, we have Shyama Ma'am's niece. She is an intern...'

'I am not an intern! I'm a licensed psychotherapist!' a young female voice hushes the receptionist.

'Madam, sorry, madam,' the receptionist says. 'Our intern is telling she's real doctor only, madam. She's studying in Australia and all.'

'I have finished studying!' Meg hears the protests. 'I just haven't started practicing yet because I'm still contemplating studying further.'

Meg is conflicted, but her gut isn't. A resounding 'yes' is what she seems to detect. So she decides to do something completely out of character and go with it. 'That's fine,' Meg says. 'Please give me an appointment as soon as possible with...'

'Ms Binny' the receptionist says. 'She's free only, madam. You can come now also.'

'God!' Meg hears Binny say. 'Just hang up quickly, please.'

'Great. Please tell Binny I'll be over at 3 p.m. today,' Meg says and hangs up.

Oh god, what am I doing, going to therapy and with a novice at that? Meg sinks into bed, trying to make sense of her new go-with-the-gut policy. Except, she's feeling irrationally positive about this despite everything. Strange.

~

Meanwhile, Tania is also making some changes to the way she's been approaching life. Perhaps it's time to take a page out of Meg's book and start taking action instead of waiting around for the cosmos to treat her well. But then again, what has taking action ever gotten Meg? Well, it did get her Neel. It's a different matter that she doesn't have the sense to see it. Yes, that's it. Tania is ready for a worldview makeover. Just as soon as she's cleansed herself of residual attachment to the past, that is. But what if Ryan was The One and she's made a terrible mistake by passively letting him move cities? What would Meg say about this? Never mind. She's done consulting other people, the tarot and the planets. She's going to make this decision for herself. If Ryan is meant to be, it will happen. But not right now. Not like this. She needs to take some time off to figure out what to do about Aditi and their company before worrying about her relationship status again. She misses Ryan, but she isn't acting on her feelings anymore. No more silly, emotional Tania. She's decided to be an adult. And a doer.

'I look forward to being an adult,' she says taking a long, hard sniff of the fabric softener.

37

'The main reason I like to test theories I don't agree with is for the sense of triumph I feel when they fail.' – Meg

Therapists in India play a secret game in their head when a new patient walks through the door. It's called 'Is This Someone Whose Entire Concept of Therapy Is Based on American Pop Culture?'. It's a very short game, though, since those patients that do fall under this category give themselves away by a visible display of shock and disappointment upon the absence of a couch.

'No couch? What? Why is there no couch?' Meg says to the eager to please Binita Nambiar who has gone out of her way to appear, well, *doctorly.*

'Ohh...yes...we should do something about that, but the rooms here are so small,' she fumbles around for a way to convince Meg that she's in fact a legit therapist. 'We had those in Perth...where I studied...just hospitals here...'

'It's the couch!' Meg is in disbelief. 'It's the centrepiece of therapy!'

'I understand,' says the inexperienced therapist, awkwardly gesturing for her to take a seat on the wooden chair available.

Thankfully, Meg obliges, scanning the small room uneasily. It has a distinct Catholic-school-headmistress-office vibe to it. But perhaps they are just being clever by inducing associations that trigger all that dark, repressed stuff, Meg wonders.

'Doctor...?' Meg tries to figure out what to call her. She looks discouragingly young.

'You can call me Binny. All my friends call me Binny,' she beams. 'Err, patients. I meant patients. Of course.'

'Binny,' Meg says in her signature no-nonsense tone. 'Before we start, let's be very clear about some things. I know that you're new at this, but I picked you not based on your qualifications or experience but because I had a feeling about you...'

Binny lights up at this. 'I'm so glad to hear you say that because...'

'Shh,' Meg says and scolds herself for shushing the therapist. This isn't going to work if she doesn't take her seriously. 'I'm sorry, I didn't mean to shush you. I just...if we're doing this, I want us to be clear. And honest.'

'Yes! Yes, of course!' Binny is very excited by the idea of her very first patient having a 'feeling' about her and the fact that she doesn't have to pretend to be more or less or anything else. So excited, in fact, that she's now hugging Meg.

'And you're hugging me,' Meg says in dismay.

'Sorry! I'm sorry! I must establish boundaries with patients, not the other way around,' Binny seems to be lecturing herself. 'But I'm not an intern, really. I'm a licensed therapist.'

'It's fine,' Meg says out of sympathy for the young woman. 'Now, please don't take that as an invitation.'

Binny stares at Meg and then laughs nervously. 'Funny! You're funny!'

'Right. I'm Meghana but everyone calls me Meg.'

'Oh, but why? Meghana is such a beautiful...'

'Because I insist.'

'Right. Right, of course. Your name, your preference.'

'So, shall we begin?' Meg says. In a way she feels a lot more comfortable than she probably would have with a 'legit therapist'. There's something refreshing about novice enthusiasm.

'Yes,' Binny makes herself comfortable in her seat and brings out her file, writing pad and puts on a pair of thick-framed glasses, looking very important.

Meg tries not to chuckle.

'Now, you should know that I am the kind of psychotherapist who works with dreams as much as with anything you bring in to this office.'

Oh god, Meg thinks to herself. *I have found myself a quack.*

'So… any recent dreams you'd like to share?'

'I don't usually dream.'

'Oh, everybody dreams at least four to six times every night…' Binny is quick to explain.

'Yes, I know. I meant I don't remember my dreams.'

'Oh, that's because you're resisting the unconscious. Don't resist the unconscious!'

'I'm what now?' Meg's slowly beginning to rethink her openness to the whole intern thing.

'Okay. So, your psyche can basically be divided into two halves: the conscious and unconscious,' Binny starts to draw the anatomy of the psyche for Meg to understand and spends the next half hour explaining it.

While Meg enjoys this little therapy session, she is also aware that this is supposed to be *her* time to talk. And Binny here is teaching psychology instead of practicing it.

'Binny,' she says with all the gentleness she can muster, 'maybe I should talk now?'

Binny looks five kinds of upset as she realizes that she's been taking a psych class on a patient's time. 'I'm sorry! I'm so sorry…'

'It's fine,' Meg smiles in the hope that it would calm her down and get her to do her job.

'It's just all the projection…' Binny says nervously.

'I'm sorry?'

'You remind me of my mother,' she blurts out and Meg's eyebrows go as high as they can. All right, she may have signed up for a fresher, but she had not signed up for a sitcom. This is so inappropriate, she cannot believe they let therapists on the loose without the basics in place.

'God, I'm doing it again!' Thankfully, she realizes this by herself this time. 'I'm sorry! That was so inappropriate. It's just so exciting to see it all come alive, you know?'

Meg remains silent. And confused.

'Sorry, you couldn't possibly know what I'm talking about. Maybe we should just start?'

'Okay. I'm just going to start talking,' Meg says and Binny nods eagerly, making every effort to keep her mouth zipped.

It lasts for a whole 20 minutes, by which time Meg has brought her up to speed on her current crises – her job, her mother, Neel, Rajeev and most importantly, the Goal. 'Wow,' Meg is impressed by the restraint Binny has shown. 'I was not betting on completing that story in this session.'

'I did it, didn't I!' Binny is thrilled with her progress. 'The way you talk about the Goal though, you really are my mother!' And she's back again.

'Crap! No! I mean, I'm sorry, I'm just nervous. I'll do better next time, I swear.'

Meg watches her in amused silence.

'There will be a next time, right?' Binny looks at Meg with sad puppy eyes.

'Relax,' Meg says. 'I have a feeling about you, remember?'

Binny beams at that. 'Thank you. For being so patient and everything. If it is okay with you, I'd like to not say anything today – I'd like to collect my thoughts and you know, reflect on everything you've shared so far and figure out a way forward.'

'Sounds good,' Meg smiles.

'But Meg,' she says as Meg reaches for the door. 'I need you to take me seriously even though we both know this is my first time and so far, I haven't really given you a reason to.'

'I do take you seriously,' Meg says.

'Then I need you to keep a dream journal. Write down your dreams, no matter how insignificant you think they may be and bring them to me. Okay?'

'But I told you – I don't remember my dreams!'

'Yes, but that can be fixed. You just have to sincerely intend to remember them and make a conscious effort. Buy a journal and keep it by your bedside. The unconscious should register your intention and you should slowly be able to remember dream fragments.'

Meg looks at her like she's in a parody. 'You're not serious…'

'Totally serious. See you next week?'

'Okay.'

'Wow,' Meg says to herself. 'Just what have I got myself into?'

38

'Theories are great. It's the practicum that fucks you up.' – Tania

It's the last week of December, a time when that soppy, taking stock, end-of-the-year feeling sets in for both Meg and Tania, who are now at lunch at a fancy restaurant discussing the complexities of their respective existences before Tania takes leave for Kodaikanal.

'How did we get here?' Tania says, sipping her mojito thoughtfully. 'What triggered all this?'

'The bet,' Meg says. 'It made us blind. This need to win started to consume us and at some point, we forgot why we were doing this in the first place – to get our lives together and now…'

'Uhh…no. I have no such need. That is entirely you. I genuinely wanted to find the love of my life and believed I could. The bet was merely motivation to keep at it and test my own theories.'

'Yeah, I just wanted to win,' Meg says through a heavy, persistent yawn.

'Not been getting sleep?' Tania asks. 'I haven't been sleeping well either.'

'No, it's actually this… this… ridiculous thing I signed up for.'

'What thing?'

'I'll tell you, but you better not tell anyone. Ever.'

'Yeah, yeah, okay! Now tell me already!'

'I'm in therapy,' Meg says, and Tania suppresses her desire to squeal with delight.

'And it's not what you think. The therapist you recommended is in the US currently, and so I'm stuck with her quack of a niece who isn't even legit. Like, I'm her first patient. She's from Australia and she's here doing this "for the experience".'

Tania's mouth is wide open. 'And you're letting her? You, Meghana Rao, stickler for experience and academic excellence, you're letting her?'

'Yes. And this is the embarrassing part: I'm letting her because of a *gut feeling*.'

Tania's eyes widen as she takes in the shocking news.

'It's just that…I've done it my way all this time… I've made plans, I've acted on them, I've botched everything up. Now, I'm trying the opposite. I'm trying to be more like you and trust the process…my gut… Oh god, what am I even doing…'

'No, no, it's great!' Tania says. 'I'm doing the same thing! I mean, I've decided to try the opposite too. I'm going to take charge, grab life by the horns, make some plans and try to consciously direct my life instead of basing everything on signs.'

'Wow, it's like we've swapped theories,' Meg says.

'Actually, we do seem to have,' Tania smiles.

'Well, here's to the swap and hoping it works,' Meg raises her glass.

'Oh, if it isn't my two favourite girls!' It's Suchi. Suchi, Tania's friend who set Meg up on a date with a guy who was in love with her. That Suchi. They haven't met or spoken since and you'd expect it to be awkward, but Suchi seems incredibly happy to see them. Almost obnoxiously happy and un-Suchi like. She also seems to have coloured her hair purple. Another un-Suchi-like move.

'Hey! Suchi!' Tania says. 'Long time!'

'Yes, I've been going through some stuff... But everything's great now and... guess what?' She wags her now bare ring finger at them. 'I'm divorced!' she says gleefully.

Meg and Tania exchange looks. They can't tell if this is the kind of glee that is followed by a breakdown or genuine happiness at finally finding the courage to do something one has put off for a very long time.

'Uhh...' Tania searches for the right thing to say.

'Congratulations!' Meg says. 'If you're happy, we're happy.' Whatever it takes to shorten this conversation so that she can go back to having lunch with her bestie who is leaving town shortly and indefinitely.

'Thanks!' Suchi pulls up a chair and makes herself comfortable. 'Oh, I'm having a "Suddenly Single" party. You two should come!'

'A what party?' Meg says.

'Suddenly single. You know? When life is going one way and you think you have everything figured out and ta-da! You're suddenly single. And you're a woman with purple hair, no attachments and too many options,' she winks.

'Right,' Tania tries to say it like she gets it while Meg is getting increasingly uncomfortable with the new and divorced Suchi.

'So, what's up with you guys? How's it going? I cannot tell you how delighted I am to join the singles club.'

Meg and Tania smile awkwardly. 'Suchi, you do remember that we don't particularly want to be in the singles club, right?' Tania says.

'Oh, right. That bet. How is that working out for you, by the way?' Suchi says. 'Any luck? I mean, I'm sure you've been on many dates by now. Has any guy made you feel like you couldn't do better on your own?'

Meg pretends to examine the menu while Tania orders another drink.

'And thank god if you haven't found that person because once you decide that one mere mortal is going to play a huge role in your personal happiness, that is the end of all happiness,' Suchi says.

'So, what happened to Tarsh?' Meg can't resist asking. She's quite sure he's the reason for Suchi's divorce given how he couldn't stop going on and on about her on their date.

'That's what I'm saying. When I got married, I thought I had found The One. For a while, it was all right. Even better than all right. And I think we could have actually had a chance of being happy if I hadn't burdened that marriage with my expectations of being with The One. No one can be The One. There is no One. There is only The Good Enough One. And since I couldn't find this, I fell into the inevitable trap of transferring my fixation on to someone else. Another guy. Someone who was unlike the one I married in every way. The Anti-One...'

Meg and Tania are riveted. The Anti-One? Wow, Suchi is ready to star in her award-winning romcom already.

'But once I left my marriage and started a real relationship with Tarsh, I could tell it's going to be a repeat of the past. Not because he wasn't good enough. He definitely was. He just wasn't The One. As no one is. So, my theory is that, you can either suck it up and make it work with any one of The Good Enough Ones, which is what most sensible people do. But if you, like me, are the kind of person who wants more out of love, of a marriage, than just a stable, functional relationship, then you're not going to be happy with The Good Enough One. So I say, screw it! Screw the need for The One. Find something else – travel, read, find a hobby, go back to college, hell, take a lover or a fictional lover. But spare yourself the disappointment of being with The One.'

Meg and Tania stare at her in frozen silence. They're going to need a few more mojitos. 'Oh hey, I saw Neel the other day,' she turns to Meg abruptly. 'Looks like he's doing really well!'

'Oh, yes, he is. His band is coming out with an album soon and he's going to be on a TV show as well. I guess doing great just about sums it up!' Meg smiles.

'Oh wow!' Suchi says. 'I had no idea. I was talking about the new woman. She seemed nice. And it's good that things are finally working out for him. I mean, we all thought he'd never get over you.'

Tania tries to make eyes at Suchi to stop talking but Suchi doesn't notice. Meg meanwhile is channelling her inner ice queen and failing. 'Uh, he's seeing someone?'

'Yeah, you didn't know? Wait. It's okay that I mentioned it right?'

'Yes...yes, yes! Of course! Why wouldn't it be? I mean...' she laughs awkwardly as Tania watches on helplessly.

'Excuse me,' Meg turns to the waiter. 'Could you please cancel that margarita and make it a tequila shot instead?'

39

'What happens in therapy stays in your bloody head and that's why it is ill advised to go to therapy in the first place.' – Meg

It is Meg's eighth session with her fresher therapist. The last few had been somewhat encouraging with Binny doing all the work and arriving at the conclusion that Meg really wanted to be with Neel but was actually afraid of marrying a man just like her father. Unfortunately, she had said so in exactly those words, which led to Meg leaving the session abruptly. But today is different. Today, Meg has a few things to say. A few decisions she needs to say out loud in the presence of an unbiased third party. Tania had offered to stay and offer comfort, what with the news of Neel dating and all that, but Meg had insisted she go home. This is something she's going to have to do alone. Uh, alone with Binny. Also, she finally has a dream to bring to the session. Yes, resistant-to-the-unconscious Meghana Rao finally remembers a dream. This has to mean she's making psychological progress. Yay.

'Meg! You showed up!' Binny is surprised to see her after how the last session went.

'Why wouldn't I…' Meg says walking in. 'Wait, something's different…'

Binny smiles, pleased with herself.

'Oh my god! Is that a *couch?*'

'Indeed it is!' Binny unveils the compact yellow couch. 'It isn't much, but I wanted to do something nice for this session, considering how the last one went...you know, in case you showed up.'

'Aww,' Meg says in spite of herself. Sometimes she can't tell who needs therapy more, and that's what she loves about Binny. She doesn't feel like a patient here.

'That is really sweet, thank you. I have a surprise for you too,' Meg says, pulling out her dream journal.

'Noooo. Really? You brought me a dream?'

'You sound like I brought you a puppy.'

'It's kind of like that,' Binny says. 'Okay, okay. Let's settle down. I want to hear everything!'

'Yes, but before that...' Meg quickly brings her up to speed on the news of Neel moving on, and Binny considers this quietly.

'So now you agree I need to move on from him?'

'On the contrary, I was waiting to hear what you were going to do about it,' Binny says.

'Do about it? What's there to do? He's moved on. Good for him. I asked him to! Now I must too. For real. For good.'

'That's it? Is there no fight in you at all? You're just going to give up?'

'Neel and I do not work. We already tried it, remember? For four whole years?' Meg raises her voice reflexively. 'We just don't work together.'

'No, that's not what I heard. You didn't work for very specific reasons which, if I may point out, no longer exist,' Binny says calmly. She's learnt a thing or two about Meg's temper and is not intimidated by it.

'That's not the point!'

'That is the point. Give me one good reason he isn't right for you.'

'Well, he's seeing someone else! If he really wanted to be with me, he'd be trying harder!'

Binny doesn't bother trying to appear like she's not appalled. 'Uh, he did. In fact, he's the only one who's been consistently trying. You, on the other hand, repeatedly pushed him away and still went running back to him when you needed him!'

'That's unfair! That happened once, and he basically insisted on playing at the launch to save my ass. I'm not responsible for his saviour complex. I didn't *make* him do anything.'

'Right. Okay. So, what's your plan now?' Binny says, arms folded and looking stern and matronly.

'The plan is to move on. I got sidetracked. With the whole Rajeev situation blowing up in my face and my mother and… I got sidetracked. I thought maybe just this once, I must do something novel and trust my gut and maybe…'

'Maybe?'

'Never mind. This was a stupid idea. I don't trust my gut. My gut is never right. I have decided to go back to doing what I do best.'

'Which is?'

'Following through on my plan, of course. I had a specific goal for this year and this year will be over soon – though, technically, I started in the middle of the year and so, I have another six months but it's this whole end-of-the-year feeling and… I cannot just sit back and let my gut take the wheel right now!'

'So what are you going to do, Meg?' Binny asks patiently.

'I'm going to start dating again. I can't let one – all right, two – disasters stop me from reaching the finish line!'

'Meg…'

'No, don't Meg me. My mind is made up. I know what I'm doing.'

Binny sighs. This is the first time in their interaction that she actually feels like a therapist. A legit one. For once, she actually knows what's going on. She also knows that Meg isn't about to listen to her until she makes it worse for herself. She feels utterly powerless in her position as the caregiver and at the same time, she feels validated because this is exactly how she's supposed to feel at this point in the therapeutic journey.

'You said you had a dream,' Binny says finally.

'Yes. The dream. Yes, let's talk about that instead.' Meg opens her journal and starts to read. 'It is night. I am in the backseat of a car which seems to be driving itself. It's frightening as hell, and I try to reach the brakes from behind as the car swerves out of control, but I can't seem to reach it. I wake up, terrified.'

Binny smiles like someone who thinks she knows exactly what the dream means but is probably not about to explain it since it wouldn't be received well.

'What? What does it mean?' Meg says, a touch nervous. It's like she suspects the dream is trying to confront her with something she isn't willing to face yet.

Binny is making her work for it.

'Look, if you know something, just say it!'

'Sorry, Meg. But I'm not going to interpret your dream. Besides, I don't think you're ready to hear what I think. You're just going to have to live this one out in order to figure it out,' Binny says.

Meg rolls her eyes, tells herself that Binny clearly has no idea what the dream means and marches off to the door.

'What's *driving* you?' Binny says as Meg reaches the door.

'Huh?' Meg says, without turning around.

'You might want to ask yourself that. Because whatever complex is driving you from within is more powerful and autonomous than you think and not that I'm an expert, but I think it is going to get you into trouble unless you address it.'

Meg stands still for just a moment to let that sink in before proceeding to do exactly as promised: move the hell on.

40

'When the going gets tough, the tough are never too tough to admit they need Mommy.' - Tania

Tania is doing her best to ignore the signs (and there have been many). In fact, she's making a deliberate effort to go in the opposite direction since going with the flow and trusting the signs is what landed her in this mess in the first place. This is it. She's reached the end of her tether. She's reached her own version of that famous crying-on-the-bathroom-floor moment from *Eat Pray Love*. And now she needs a plan. And since she can't afford to travel to three exotic countries and follow it up with an internationally bestselling memoir, she is all set with packed bags (and goat) to go to Kodaikanal just in time for New Year's Eve with her mother. And everything will fall in place once there because her mother, aka the Woman Who Knows, will make her problems disappear by giving her exactly the solution she needs.

'Mehhhhhhhh!' Elsa protests as Tania loads her in her hatchback at 7 a.m. She has been trying to tell her (as clearly as goats can) that she does not approve of this plan, but Tania has been too self-absorbed to notice.

'You're going to be fine, Elsa,' Tania says. 'We're going to be fine, I promise. In fact, we are at the precipice of dramatic change,'

Tania says, locking the doors. 'This is the part of the romcom where the heroine sets out to find herself and returns with her own version of happily ever after. This is when the story really moves forward!'

Elsa rolls her eyes. It's just like Tania to make this about herself. In fact, it almost feels like the only reason she adopted her was because no one would listen to her whine about her love life.

Tania turns on the radio as she passes by what used to be the street Ryan lived on. 'Never mind, I'll find someone like youuuuuu,' Adele sounds whinier than ever, blaring out of the speakers. 'Are you serious?' Tania grunts at her own playlist, switches it off and turns on the radio. Elsa snorts. 'Now you're just somebody that I used to know,' sings Gotye. 'You have got to be kidding me!' Tania turns off the radio. 'What's with all the break up songs? *God*.'

'*Mehh mehhhhhh mehh!*' Elsa tries to point out that it was Tania's idea to let Ryan move on and that if it bothers her so much, she should just get in touch with him. But Tania is too preoccupied to listen. They drive the rest of the way – and it's a long way, more than half a day – with Tania bursting into short rants every half hour while Elsa attempts to get a word in edgeways.

It's about 8 p.m. when Tania reaches Kodaikanal. The house smells of freshly-baked fig and honey cake that brings back fond memories of her childhood. It's just like her mother to ensure her visit is perfect from the minute she sets foot inside the house.

'Tanu!' Mrs Rebello comes out to meet her. She's a short, pudgy woman who looks like she's made entirely of love and sponge cake.

'Hi!' Tania collapses in her arms though she's clearly too tall to stay that way.

'*Mehhhh!*' Elsa doesn't like being left out.

'Well, hello there, you must be Elsa!' Mrs Rebello greets her new visitor and decides to show her the garden, which is beautifully lit with decorative lights. Elsa approves. This place is so much greener than godforsaken Chennai. Ooh, and colder. 'My plants better be alive when I come out!' Mrs Rebello calls out to Elsa as she takes Tania in and insists on overfeeding her immediately.

'Can I talk now before the year ends?' Tania says, stretching her tired legs into her mother's lap on the other end of the futon in the living room at about 10 p.m., after dinner, a shower and the traditional tour of the garden are all done.

'I think so,' says a very pleased Mrs Rebello, and Tania brings her up to speed on everything from Ryan to Aditi and is surprised to note that her mother isn't even remotely shaken up by any of it

'Well...?'

'Well, what?'

'Well, say something! React! Your daughter's life has fallen apart!'

'Don't be dramatic,' Mrs Rebello smiles fondly at her daughter. 'You just have to work things out with Aditi, that's all.'

'Uhh, that's *all*? Did you not hear the part where she won't talk to me? Where she's so angry, she basically threw me out? And what about my non-existent love life? I mean, am I ever going to have that? What you and Dad had?'

'Baby...' Mrs Rebello says in the voice of the Woman Who Knows. 'It's not like you to just give up on your friend. Work it out with Aditi. You'll find a way. Give it time and don't lose your mind over it. It's going to be fine, she's hurt and she is showing it differently than you would.'

'Fine. But I need you to be a normal parent and start looking for a guy for me.'

Mrs Rebello laughs. 'What?' And then she realizes that Tania's serious. 'Baby…'

'No. Don't "baby" me. Don't tell me that this isn't how it works, and I can't force a meeting with my soulmate.'

'Well, I don't know that. I just know that you have a narrow definition of what a soulmate might be.'

'No, no, no, no, no and no. Don't give me that Meg could be your soulmate and I could be your soulmate crap,' Tania says. 'I want romance and sunsets and soulful stirrings and – just no. This can't be it.'

Mrs Rebello smiles affectionately. 'But what if you had what I had, and it was taken away from you in 20 years? Would that be better?'

Tania looks like she hadn't considered this before. 'No. But stop doing that! Stop making true love look tragic. Like I can't have a soulmate unless I'm prepared to lose him or something.'

'I'm not saying that. I'm just saying, we might all choose different stories for ourselves if we had the chance to. Or we just might find that the one we have is the best version. But either way, baby…'

'I should stop trying to make things happen.'

'Yes.'

'But are you saying taking action is wrong?'

'Of course not. I'm just saying that you will not like anyone I might find if I put the word out. And since you're a believer in dreams and magic, you must remain true to that.'

'Meaning?'

'Meaning, take some time to heal and then go back to trusting your gut.'

'But...but what about Ryan?'

'You'll see how he fits in eventually,' Mrs Rebello kisses her daughter goodnight at the stroke of midnight and leaves the room for Tania to open the new year pondering their conversation more deeply before retiring into the bedroom.

'I hate it when she does that,' Tania says to herself as she realizes that everything her mother just said makes perfect sense.

41

'I wonder if this thing we call falling in love is simply what a psychologist might call falling into a complex – an attempt to find the unknown, disowned parts of us in others.' – Meg

It is their tenth session, and Meg and Binny sit cross-legged, facing each other in hostile silence. Binny drums her fingernails on the arm rest of her chair while Meg pretends to study the ceiling. The passive-aggressiveness in the room is palpable given how the last session went. In fact, Meg had decided she was quitting therapy and that the whole thing was a terrible idea that had come upon her in a moment of desperation. Binny had tried to do the mature thing and called her to have a civilized conversation (at precisely that time), and Meg had been anything but civil. So, if this session is going weirdly, it's because both parties have reached what they call transference and counter-transference in psychoanalysis – when the patient and the therapist are caught up in an unconscious dance where they project their issues and inner conflicts on to each other. And since this is our therapist's very first patient, she hasn't been able to catch it early on as therapists normally do.

'Fine, I'll talk. I'm the therapist. What brings you here? I thought you were "quite done with this idiocy" and already knew what you were going to do next?'

'Yes, but I'm not here to discuss Neel. I've found a job. In Mumbai. For the kind of role that anyone in my position would kill for, for a bigger company with bigger clients and a much bigger paycheck.'

'So, what's the problem?' Binny says like someone who knows exactly what the problem is, and this sets off Meg.

'You know, this is it. This is my problem with you – why do you do that?'

'Do what?' Binny genuinely does not know what Meg's talking about.

'This whole "asking questions while you know the answer all along" thing. It's bloody irritating and passive-aggressive.'

'First of all, I do not know what I'm doing to make you think that but now that we've established that I am passive-aggressive, shall we move on to your problems?'

Meg rolls her eyes.

'That book you were writing. What happened to it?' Binny says, ignoring Meg's obvious resistance to the subject.

'What happened? Nothing happened. It's safe in the drawer – where it belongs.'

'Well, are you working on it?'

'Look, let's be very clear. I'm not working on it. It's more like a hobby. I mentioned that only because you kept prying about my "other interests". I would never give up the security of a stable career for something as fickle and egocentric as a creative pursuit. I'm simply not that irresponsible!'

'Right,' Binny's got her analytical face on. 'Tell me again how you felt about your father abandoning you and your mother to pursue his art.'

'Okay. I hate everything my father stood for. That is not a secret. And it does not take a shrink to figure that out. So please, before you pat yourself on your smug little back for this major therapeutic breakthrough, let me point out that I have always known this, and I continue to stand by what I know. I don't just resent artistic pursuits because of my father, but because artists as a breed are egocentric, irresponsible, overgrown babies who think the world owes them a living!' Meg suddenly realizes that she's on her feet and yelling.

'Got it,' Binny says calmly, handing Meg a glass of water which she begrudgingly takes.

'I'm sorry, I didn't mean to yell,' she says after taking a few minutes to sit down and regain her composure.

'Don't apologize. It means we're making progress,' Binny smiles.

'We are?'

'Tell me about the job. What's the problem? Why aren't you jumping at the offer?'

'Well, I am jumping at the offer! It's just...I won't have a life apart from it, should I take it up. And that would have been all right even last year but now... I just can't help this nagging insistence at the back of my head that life should be... more! It's almost embarrassing because it's not like I can define that concretely and I need everything defined, you know?'

'I know.'

'And my mother's here and I'd have to move...'

'But I thought you and your mother weren't...'

'No. I mean, yes, you're right, we aren't speaking right now...'

'But you hope to make amends and get into her good books again,' Binny says.

'Yes...no. Wait...what?' Meg is showing all the signs of losing her composure again and is now beginning to suspect that Binny might be setting her up for it. 'You think I need my mother's approval?'

'I don't know, Meg. You tell me. You say you've had a difficult relationship with your mother all your life. That you've found her overbearing, critical and emotionally distant. And while you've managed to build a separate life for yourself, telling yourself all along that you're nothing like her, all your choices say otherwise. You find a reason to break ties with anyone who even vaguely reminds you of your dad and challenges your resistance to a different point of view. You approach life like it is only facts and figures and there is no room for any sloppiness, either your own or others'. You told yourself that the arranged marriage route might be for you though it is so unlike you. Even after it blew up in your face and your mother had no business putting pressure on you in the first place, you feel the need to make things right with her. You know better than to take up a job that will give you no room to have a life, but you're worried it would invite her wrath all over again. Should I keep going?'

Meg is very quiet. There's a hint of tears in the corners of her eyes but she successfully holds them all back. 'The job is not about her,' she says after a while.

'What is it about then?'

'The book – how do I know I'll be any good at it if I tried?' Meg surprises herself with this blatant display of vulnerability. 'I can't fail. I can't…I can't fail because if I do, then I'd have to rely on someone else. And I can't put myself through that.' Now, she's crying.

'How long have you been writing this book?' Binny asks, leaning forward.

'I don't know. Two years. Maybe three. I don't know.'

'Will you do something even though it might be totally out of character for you?'

'You're going to ask me to ditch the job…'

'No. No it's not about the job. I'm asking you to complete the book. Just for the sake of writing it. Not because it would lead to a book deal or change your life in any way. I just want you to direct all your focus and energy into writing a really good book. And when you're done, let it go. Don't keep at it over and over. Can you do that?'

'Yes, but what about the job?'

'What is the next step with the job? Do you have to accept it immediately?'

'No, I'd have to go to Mumbai and meet a few people but after that, yes, it's pretty much a matter of accepting or declining, I guess.'

'Okay. Buy yourself as much time as possible while directing all your energy into the book and for the sake of writing a good book. Nothing more, nothing less. No thinking about the job or your mother or your future or the many things that could go wrong should you pursue a creative calling. Okay?'

'Okay, but…'

'But nothing. Just do this and let's meet when you're done. Unless there's an emergency in between.'

'Okay.'

Binny beams like a proud mama. 'We've made massive progress today, Meg.'

Meg musters a sincere smile. She is glad they're making psychological progress. But how long is it going to take to make some concrete progress in her outer life, damn it?

42

'I feel the genre of my life switching from romcom to psych thriller, and not in a good way.' – Tania

It's only been a few days since Tania took her mother's advice, decided to let go, be herself, and things are already looking up. Or maybe it's the whole birth of the new year thing. For starters, Aditi has sent her a text saying that perhaps she had overreacted and not considered her feelings and intentions and that while this didn't mean 'things are cool', she was writing to say that she needs some time and space. This is good. It's progress and quite unexpected at that. Tania has replied saying she needs some time and space too. It's nice being reached out to by someone for a change. To have nothing to get done in a day and to simply drown herself in whatever activity feels most soothing. It's just the thought of the entire closet of tarot and oracle cards that are never coming back that keeps her up at night these days.

'How could I do that? I mean, I could have given them to someone to keep for me or given them away to someone who might use them. How could I just discard them so thoughtlessly? I am so incapable of thinking calmly, it's just...'

'You are passionate,' her mother says. 'It's what makes you "you". You feel everything intensely, and you're driven by your feelings. There's nothing wrong with that.'

'Yes, but I really want those cards now,' Tania groans.

'Maybe it's time to move on from that. Maybe you don't need those cards anymore. Maybe you're just looking for ways to take responsibility for how you feel.'

'What do I feel?' Tania asks and Mrs Rebello laughs.

'Okay, I'm not going to figure *everything* out for you,' she says on her way out of Tania's bedroom.

'Mom?' Tania calls out like she always did as a child every time her mother started to leave the room.

'Yes, baby?' Mrs Rebello says.

'I miss Ryan.'

Mrs Rebello doesn't say anything but takes a seat on the cane chair with all the freshly laundered clothes on it.

'I mean, I know I should let it go and it's actually kind of absurd that I'm even taking it so seriously. I mean, nothing even happened! But I can't brush away how I felt the entire time. Like... we've known each other all along. Like he was in every way the soulmate I have craved all my life...'

Mrs Rebello listens intently without giving away even a hint of how she's receiving any of this. It's one of the superpowers of the Woman Who Knows.

'I know what you're going to say, that I want a soulmate so much that I'm forcing this to be The One.'

'I'm not saying anything,' Mrs Rebello says.

'But I just can't shake it off, Mom. I'm trying but I can't. I actually made him leave. I told myself I was mad at him and I had every reason to be. And to be fair, he was kind of a coward and I don't even understand why I still want him...'

'Call him. Simple.'

'What? That's it? You don't have any wise words for me? No telling me that it worked out as it was supposed to and that I must go with the flow?'

'Baby,' Mrs Rebello says affectionately. 'Going with the flow does not mean you ignore your feelings. Your feelings are valid, and they're trying to tell you something.'

'So...I should call him. Just like that.'

'Just like that.'

'Well it's been weeks and since he has made no attempt to reach out, he's probably moved on as well. Also, he's not on social media, so it's not like I can casually get in touch with him or find out what's up.' Tania buries herself under a stack of pillows.

'Can you just call him, please? If you don't get through, we'll accept that it isn't meant to be. What do you say?'

Tania slowly emerges from under the pillow pile. 'Okay,' she says faintly, picking up her phone. She searches through her contacts and comes across Ryan's name saved as Ryan Virus. She smiles, thinking of Virus and their first run-in, and proceeds to hit the call button and her heart rate picks up. 'God, I can't,' she disconnects immediately. 'I mean, what am I even going to say?'

'Since when has my daughter worried about what she'd say? Come on, you're the queen of spontaneity. What's happened to you?'

'Life. Life has happened to me, Mom. As you can see, my spontaneity has got me into quite a bit of trouble.'

'You don't know that yet. And besides, if you ask me, I think it's the overthinking that's been getting in the way and not the spontaneity,' Mrs Rebello says.

'I wish I had your confidence!'

'Stop making excuses and make that call instead. Now!'

'Okay, okay. Here goes.' Tania takes a deep, nervous breath. 'If it goes through, great. If it doesn't, no problem, because it's not like I expected anything to happen in the first place.'

'You seem to have dialled a wrong number!' It's the voice of the annoying Vodafone lady, crushing her hopes and dreams all at once. Tania takes another deep breath and hangs up. Worry lines appear on Mrs Rebello's face as she joins her daughter on the bed and wraps an arm around her.

'So...' she says.

'So...this is it,' Tania confirms. 'He's changed his number. He's moved on. Given that there is no real need to change numbers these days except to avoid someone, I should probably move on too.'

'But at least now you know for sure,' Mrs Rebello says. 'No one said closure was easy.'

The two remain in a tight embrace for a while and Tania begins to sob many months' worth of pent-up emotions. 'What if it never happens for me? I want to be okay with that. I want to be one of those strong, independent women who don't care if they have a partner, but why do I want this so much?'

'Wanting a deep love does not make you any less strong. Please don't let anyone tell you that,' Mrs Rebello says. 'And whether it will ever happen or when it will, I don't know. Apparently, I don't have all the answers. But I do know that you must go with the flow. Your flow. What's right for you. You must listen to yourself more.'

'My *self* wants him. It wants Ryan,' Tania sobs. 'This is so humiliating. Wanting someone I barely know, someone who seems to have moved on from me – it's humiliating.'

'On the contrary, it makes you that much stronger. Don't ever apologize for how much you love.'

'Stop saying wise things!' Tania breaks into a new fit of tears. 'Just be miserable with me!'

'Oh, sorry!' Mrs Rebello takes her daughter's flowing hair in her hands and braiding it. 'Life is so unfair! And this is all so, so saaaaad.'

'Like you mean it!' Tania decides to remain in this foetal position, letting her mother braid her hair.

43

'Meaningful coincidences – if they do exist – can really fuck you up.' – Meg

Three months later

Tania's mother always said that good things and bad things come in threes. They had three dogs (in all) since Tania was about seven years old, moved three houses (all lovely ones with the nicest neighbours and landlords), had three memorable holidays. Tania also had three serious falls as a child (a fact Meg attributes to her off-centre worldview), three trips to the emergency room and three school switches. That's not all. Mrs Rebello has always insisted that three months is the perfect amount of time to test anything – a belief, an arrangement, a relationship, a job. The Three-Month Rule never lies, a conviction she's managed to pass on to her daughter who has passed it on to many people since childhood, Meg being one of them.

In the last three months, our heroines have made some massive progress in their lives. Meg has finished the third chapter of her mystery novel and has actually managed to say no to the Mumbai job, though they've insisted on keeping the offer open. She has also (much against her therapist's advice) been using a certain questionable dating app and actually managed to find someone who seems to be promising if a touch mysterious (he is still Rayman78). She hasn't, until today (on the completion of three months), considered taking it any further.

And while she and Tania have been in touch the whole time, she has carefully avoided giving Tania details about Rayman78 and the fact that she now has a profile on a dating app because Tania, being Tania, would make it a much bigger deal than it needs to be.

Meanwhile, Tania has been going with the flow and helping out at a neighbourhood pre-school and has become the town sweetheart. And as gratifying as this is at many levels, she misses her old life, her real job, Aditi and Meg, and wants to return to Chennai soon.

She has also managed to accept the Ryan sub-plot as essential for her personal growth, and while she still can't seem to shake him off, she has decided to take this time to know herself better.

'All right, let's do this' Meg gives herself a pep talk to find the courage to move things forward with her new e-man. She had planned on taking this slow, but it's been three months and Meg wouldn't be Meg if she didn't move the story forward. She quickly types out her text, checks for typos and hits send:

> It's been interesting, these three months. We should meet. In the very least, I'd like to know your real name, where you live and what you do.

She waits for that familiar anxiety to catch up with her but nothing. She feels entirely at peace with this decision. It seems, the universe agrees that it's time she had these basic questions answered as well. But four hours later when the text isn't answered, she has to admit her inner equilibrium is a touch disturbed. Okay, a lot disturbed. Thoughts of Neel, his rebound girl and the Mumbai job are coming at her like a speeding train, and she tries desperately to get out of its way by throwing herself into chapter four of her novel. But the chapter must end at some point, and there is only so much writing energy one has for a day. She must discuss this with someone if she is to avoid sending another humiliating text or worse, end up calling Neel. She texts Tania instead and tells her she needs to talk right away. Tania is on Skype within the next ten minutes.

'What happened? Are you okay?' Tania panics even before Meg can get her earphones on.

'Yes, it's just…'

'Neel? You spoke to him? Oh my god, is he marrying her? You *have* to stop them!'

'You're doing it again,' Meg says and makes the face she always makes when Tania insists on rushing in with her questions without letting Meg speak.

'Sorry, sorry, go on!' Tania looks like she might explode from the suspense. In her defence, Meg's text did say that there was something she hadn't told her and needs to talk to her about it now.

'So, you remember how I was considering the whole dating app thing a long time ago?'

'Yes, but you prudishly backed out as usual. Right?' There's a gleam of expectation in Tania's eyes. 'Shut up! You found someone there? Shut up!'

'Right. So. There's this guy,' Meg begins and Tania cozies up to the screen, elbows on her knees, palms on her cheeks, like it's story time. And it is. 'Actually, at this point, I'm not even sure it's a guy,' Meg says. 'I mean, it could be anyone. A woman, an eighty-year-old perv. We've been exchanging messages and there's a nice...vibe about him. And I like chatting with him. And he gets punctuation...'

'Wow,' Tania says. 'And you met him on this app?'

'Yes! I know, right? Anyway. He's adorably awkward and has this old-world charm about him that I so love. But he hasn't even told me his real name yet. Or where he lives. Or what he does. And I don't have his number either, 'cause we only talk on the app. It was intriguing initially but now it's three months and I just...'

'Yes, of course! It's three months! It's time. You should totally ask him!' Tania says. 'In fact, you should meet!'

'Yes, well, I sent him a message this morning saying exactly that and there's been silence since.'

'What is his response time usually like?'

'Instant. Except once in the beginning when his phone had died.'

'Uh, oh.'

'Yep.'

'But maybe that's it. His phone died. Or he's just caught up with something earth-shattering. Maybe his mother fell sick. Or he dropped his phone in the toilet. Or he's sick and resting. Or his Wi-Fi is acting up and his 4G sucks. Or he's got a work meeting that has taken all day. Or he's on a flight – a long one.' Tania rattles off excuses like friends who desperately want you to be happy tend to do.

Meg sighs. 'Thanks, but I just needed to talk.'

'What does your shrink think about all this?' Tania says.

'Haven't seen her in a while. Plus, she doesn't approve. Thinks I should get it right with Neel,' Meg says.

'Well that makes two of...'

'Shh. Don't say it' Meg says. 'I need you on my side right now.'

Ting. It's the much-awaited sound of a text, and it makes both women jump. Meg leaps out of bed and grabs her phone from her desk. 'It's him,' she says to the laptop screen.

'What does it say?' Tania asks impatiently as Meg reads and slowly processes the message.

'Well?' Tania says to Meg's frozen face. 'Share!'

> `I'm Ryan. I live in Pune as of now. And I run a diner of sorts. Also, I just realized, this makes us Meg Ryan.`

Meg reads the message out loud again, disbelief in her voice. 'You did mention that your Ryan went back to Pune, right?' she says finally but Tania is quiet.

'Maybe it isn't him. I mean, he says he runs a diner.' Meg says, despite the feeling in the pit of her stomach that insists otherwise.

'His family runs a diner that his sister was managing,' Tania says after a few seconds. She looks every bit as pale and confused as Meg. 'We're seeing or involved with the same guy *again?*' she says to Meg but appears to be spacing out. 'Except we're not actually seeing him, so we can save ourselves the confrontation and the humiliation.'

'No. I'm not seeing him. Look, this means nothing. I'm totally bowing out,' Meg says, but Tania isn't listening.

'I think I'm going to be very sick. I'll talk to you later?' she ends the call.

Meg is left staring at the message and the empty screen, wondering what the odds of such a thing happening to the same people twice are. And if there just might be such a thing as a meaningful coincidence. And if so, what could this one be saying to them?

44

'If Meg Ryan isn't a sign, I don't know what is. But what if my obsession with signs is a sign of my degenerating mental health?'
– Tania

Tania has been quietly processing the shit storm that hit her three days ago and has reached the surprising conclusion that this might be the universe's way of settling their bet. Yes, their one chance at really getting to the bottom of this fate (or faith) versus determinism mystery. Also, she has conceded that it isn't Ryan's fault for moving on. She practically ordered him to. And it's not like anything has even happened yet. They're just chatting. It's a digital relationship. No, not a relationship. A digital flirtation. Actually, it's not even that considering how bad both Ryan and Meg are at flirtation. So, there isn't anything to be upset about. Or angry about. Though she can't help but notice that this would make them Meg Ryan. *Meg Ryan!* Only the queen of romantic comedy. If that's not a sign, then what is?

Tania has been exploring astrology with renewed interest ever since her mother advised her to stick to being who she is, and she's discovered this exciting predictive tool called solar arc theory, and it seems to be freakishly accurate in describing the major events of her life so far. It seems to be suggesting that a major positive turnaround in her love life is about to occur right about…now. Of course, even astrology can't tell her if that would be Ryan or someone else, but she can't seem to fight the curiosity. For once, this is more about needing the verdict to the bet than the immediate need for a partner. Check it out: they have both met the same guy. One by chance and following a sign, and the other by conscious action towards a pre-determined outcome. 'This is it,' she tells herself as she hunts for her phone under the blankets so she can text Meg at last.

> I want you to go ahead with Ryan exactly as you would have. He doesn't have to know anything. How this works out will tell us who wins the bet.

Meg is buried in her book when she receives the text. She doesn't check her phone when she writes as a matter of policy, but she's been obsessing about this whole Tania–Ryan situation. And to make matters worse, Ryan has been messaging her asking when she's visiting! What is she supposed to say to that? She's going to need to talk to Tania about that, and Tania has made it quite clear that she needs some alone time. And ghosting isn't her thing especially since she's the one who brought up the whole 'It's time we met' topic with Ryan. And while she hates to admit it, she's itching to find out who Ryan would go for if she never told him about Tania. Not because she wants to steal her best friend's guy but so that she'd finally have the answer to this stupid bet and she can go back to her life. Is that heartless and completely batshit crazy? To be thinking about a bet when your friend is dealing with a heartbreak? Yes, it is, she has decided, which is why she's directing all her focus on her book and avoiding the world and Ryan. So you see why she can't help grabbing the phone when she sees that it's Tania?

'Whoa!' Meg says as she reads the text. She had expected five kinds of responses but this she had not seen coming.

Meg: Who is this and where is Tania?
Tania: Lol. Just want to get this over with - if that makes sense.
Meg: It makes complete sense. Just not Tania-sense. Hence. Are you okay?
Tania: Really? So, you're game? And yes, I'm okay.
Meg: Of course I'm game. Why wouldn't I be? I've been all about winning the bet from the start. You're the weak one who'd let feelings get in the way.
Tania: Well, I'm done with all that. I've surrendered. Let's dp this.
Meg: To be clear...Dp this?
Tania: No, no...autocorrect. Dp this.
Meg: ?
Tania: Ufff... DO this. Let's do this!

Meg spends the next few hours intermittently chatting with Ryan, exchanging photographs and what-not. She isn't sure right at this moment if she's excited that this conversation is going so well or if it's only about the bet, or if it's all just a massive defence against being sucked into the emotional vortex that is Neel but she'll have to figure that out later. There is also a momentary prick of the conscience as she ponders about how this might affect Ryan. After all, what would happen once he finds out? How is he going to be okay with either of them? This just sounds like the beginning of a romcom that's doomed to fail. But Meg wouldn't be Meg if she couldn't silence an inconvenience like her conscience, and she proceeds with her plans with her eyes on the Goal. Or at this point, the Verdict. But there is one more thing she must do if the day is to feel completely satisfying.

~

'You don't have an appointment today!' Binny says as Meg barges into her office.

'It's fine, I'm not here for a session. I just have to tell you something,' she beams.

Binny opens her mouth to say something, but Meg is too excited to let her speak. She breathlessly reports all the recent happenings on the Meg–Ryan–Tania front and Binny's mouth is now open for completely different reasons. 'Okay. That's all I wanted to say. Bye!' Meg turns around to leave.

'No...wait!'

'Like I said, I'm not here for a session, I'm only here to gloat. Or something like it. That the whole not-going-back to Neel thing is actually working out just fine for me. Don't waste your breath on this is all I'm saying. Tania and I are both determined to do it this way.'

'Well, Tania isn't my patient so I'm only going to address you. What do you think is going to happen when you go and meet him?'

'I don't care.'

'Really? If he picked you, it would only be about the bet? You don't have any feelings for him at all?'

Meg pauses but quickly decides this isn't the time for pausing. 'I don't know. I guess I'll be happy I found The One too. I don't know. I really like him if that's what you're asking. But do I know if he's The One? No, I do not. But I'm not wired that way anyway.

I don't believe in such things. If that's all you wanted to say, I think I'll be on my way out.'

'Have you watched those movies where the hero starts dating this woman but the whole point of that woman is just to remind him that she's not the one he's supposed to be with?'

'Shut up.'

'You are that woman. Just saying.'

But Meg is already walking down the hallway by then.

45

'Synchronicity – a wink from the universe or just a twitchy eye?'
– Tania

Tania is understandably having second thoughts after bravely asking Meg to go out with Ryan. What if this whole thing was orchestrated by the universe for her to find Ryan again? And what if she had read the signs wrong and missed the boat yet again? Tania tries not to panic, but it's impossible considering what's at stake. It isn't just about missing the boat but the thought of her best friend getting on that very boat. *Ohgodohgodohgod!* Tania checks the time. There's still another three hours before Meg gets on that flight. She sits herself down on the floor, legs crossed and tries to focus on her breathing, but her heart chakra seems to be spinning like a Tora Tora. All she can think about is dramatically charging onto the scene and stopping Meg, screaming '*Nahiiiiiiin!*' like an '80s Bollywood heroine. 'Please show me a sign, please show me a sign, please show me a sign…' she says under her breath, her eyes closed. 'I just want to know if I should stop Meg and go to Pune myself. Please show me a clear sign, pleeeeeaaaasee!'

The phone rings making Tania jump. It's Aditi. There's more news. It turns out that Ryan, as a parting gift to Tania, had made things right just before leaving for Pune by explaining to Aditi that it was all his fault, but she had stubbornly insisted on being mad at Tania. But now the mighty Meera Anand, who is finally back from a long holiday to celebrate her sister breaking up with Ryan, has decided that Ever After is her lucky charm, seeing that she's been trying to get her sister to break up with him for forever now and it finally happened thanks to Tania. So as a thank-you gesture, she has decided to direct a big wedding in her circle to them but only after issuing her customary threats to end their careers should something go wrong! Aditi is very emotional and apologetic and squealing with delight all at the same time. She wants Tania to return right away (if she'd still have her as her business partner) so they can return to all the exciting work that's before them. But Tania is very silent. She's processing.

'Tania? Are you there? Please tell me you're there and the line didn't just get disconnected because I just told you a very long, emotional stor...'

'I'm here,' Tania says at last. 'This is amazing!' she tries to work up the excitement, but she can't seem to shake off the heaviness in her chest. This is her sign. 'I'll be there in a couple of days max. We'll talk then.' She quickly hangs up with Aditi and proceeds to prepare herself to let go of Ryan once and for all now that she's received her second, most definite sign. She has to go back to Chennai. To life as it used to be. Synchronicity is taking her away from Ryan, not towards him. First, Meg. Then, Meg Ryan. And now, this? Refusing to accept this sign would be nothing short of denial, and Tania has promised herself to trust the signs and stick to the plan even when it hurts because she's learnt enough to know that this is how it works. But it isn't just Ryan any more. She's kind of got used to having her mom around too.

'I don't get this whole synchronicity thing,' Mrs Rebello says.

'Something about this just feels very wrong. You say it's a wink from the universe but somehow, it feels like a twitchy eye.'

'Haww!' Tania puts her arm around her mother and gives her shoulders a squeeze. 'I'm going to miss you big time too.'

They sit in silence for a while. 'Do you have to leave tonight?' her mother asks. 'I thought we could sit out here tonight, drink hot chocolate and marshmallows, and talk about nothing.'

'Okay. One more night. I'll leave in the morning.'

'Okay.'

Meanwhile in Pune

Meg takes a deep breath as she gets off the flight. She closes her eyes and tries to tune in to her gut. Meg is certain she doesn't have gut feelings, only persistent thoughts that emanate from the frontal lobe. And right now, said thoughts are telling her that she's doing the right thing. She's taking the next logical step. And Tania making peace with Aditi and moving back to Chennai is confirmation that she's quite possibly on the right track. Except there's a faint glimmer of an idea that seems to be flickering in the general vicinity of her heart. The idea is that this whole thing comes crashing down, and Neel shows up out of the blue like the hero always does in the movies and sweeps her off her feet.

But Meg chalks this down to an overproduction of oxytocin, causing her to bond deeply with anyone she's had sex with, and it's confusing her into thinking that he must surely be The One. She puts out the flicker and calls Tania, to ask her one last time if she's totally okay with this, but there is no answer. Taking this as tacit approval from the universe, Meg walks in the direction of Ryan's diner and into what she hopes will be the final act, or at least the inciting incident, leading to the final act of this very long and tiring love story.

It's a busy diner, mostly filled with people making a quick stop on their way to work. Just like Luke's diner in *Gilmore Girls*. Meg has never seen herself with someone like Luke (she *is* Luke) but she likes the idea of being Lorelai for a change. She immediately paints a mental picture of herself living here, making herself at home, finishing her book and waking up to a man who can cook, in this cozy little town swarming with young people. But this reverie is interrupted by Ryan standing right in front of her, asking her if he can get her anything. It takes Meg a few seconds to realize that Ryan hasn't recognized her from her profile picture. He's quickly moved on to fetch something for someone else, and Meg is now anxious about not being as attractive as her display picture.

'Uhh, you must be Ryan,' she says tentatively as he returns to ask her what she'd like again. She immediately realizes how stupid that must sound considering that this is a diner named Ryan's and he's the only one behind the counter.

'Nicely deduced,' he smiles. It's a good smile, Meg notes. Teeth in a row, no coffee stains. 'What can I get you?'

Meg is thrown. Surely, she couldn't be this hard to recognize? And it's not like she just showed up here unannounced. 'Ryan, it's me, Meg!'

Now it's his turn to look disoriented. He looks at her blankly for a second without saying anything. 'Meg?'

'Yeah!'

A moment's silence and a flicker of recognition. 'Ah, Meg Ryan! I get it!' he laughs but it sounds like nervous laughter. And when Meg doesn't say anything, he has to admit, 'Okay, I don't get it.'

'Unbelievable!' Meg says. By now, she's convinced he's just

playing hard to get. And yet, there's something genuinely, well, *genuine* about the guy – one of those people you instinctively trust and you don't know why. Maybe this is what they call gut feelings? Ryan does not seem to know who she is. 'Meg? The dating app? We've been exchanging messages for the last three months, and you invited me over to finally meet up?' By now, all the ears around them perk up. Sensing major drama based entirely on a misunderstanding about to unfold, Ryan quickly walks over to Meg from behind the counter and asks if they can find a different spot to talk. They walk out of the diner, all eyes still on them.

'I'm so sorry,' Ryan says once they're out of earshot and he sounds sincere. 'But I don't have the slightest idea what you're talking about.'

Meg is upset and embarrassed (embarrassed mostly) but believes him for some reason and brings him up to speed. It takes Ryan a few minutes, but he manages to connect the dots. This was his sister's doing. It had to be. This wouldn't be the first time she'd created a profile for him on a dating app. 'I'm so sorry,' he says when it hits him. 'She has no sense of boundaries, and she's always trying to fix my life in her twisted but well-meaning way. This isn't the first time she's tried to set me up behind my back, but she seems to have taken it to a whole other level here!'

Ryan is furious you can tell and for some reason, Meg finds that her own annoyance slash disappointment is quickly dissipating into some form of relief. It's like a part of her has been waiting to hear exactly this. Like she's always known that this wasn't quite it, but she needed more than signs and the advice of trusted friends. She needed things to actually happen. She needed facts. She needed to hear it from the horse's mouth. She needed to know in no uncertain or abstract terms that she was on the wrong lane. Now she's free to go after the one thing she's wanted the whole time. 'No, no, don't worry about it!' She can't help sounding happy and a little hyper, though she understands how this might be really confusing for poor Ryan. 'This worked out great!'

'It did?' Ryan is not sure what to think right now.

'You need to talk to Tania!'

'Tania…?'

'Yes, crazy dog training lady you fell in love with? That Tania!'

'What? How do you…wait…'

'God! Keep up. We don't have time for this. Anyway, she was upset about the whole dating app thing because of course we both assumed it was you talking to me this whole time, and she concluded you were probably totally over her even though she basically asked you to move on. She hasn't quite moved on from you but because she's neurotic and believes in signs, she wanted me to go ahead and meet you and… I'm talking too fast – I'm sorry but I'm having all these realizations in one go and it's a bit too much, and you need to talk to Tania. You might want to get on that plane back to Chennai with me right now!'

Ryan feels like he's just been told he's in the *Matrix*, but that there's a way out and there's no time to think and he's just going to have to trust this small, somewhat scary lady who showed up out of nowhere to give him the news.

'You want to sit somewhere?' he says for lack of anything else to say.

'No, Ryan! There's no time to sit! I must go to Chennai right away to go claim the love of my life and save him from a potentially disastrous relationship decision. And from the looks of it, so do you! If you know what's best for you, you'll jump on the plane with me and I can fill you in on everything. Or, you can do the safe, cautious grown-up thing, stay here, waste another two to three years seeing different people before you realize that Tania is The One and take that flight to Chennai anyway. And if you're really lucky, she'll still be single. Or by then, she would've made a dumb decision of her own and started seeing someone totally wrong for her. And then you'd have to wait around for her to see the light, end that relationship, and by then, you'd have both wasted another five to six years. Your choice. But I've decided I'm too damn old to be wasting anymore time vacillating because modern romance is fucked up and I don't want to be fucked up, Ryan. I want my big love. I want the rest of my life to be one grand series finale.'

Ryan stares back in frightened silence. 'Can I at least go and fetch my sister so she can take charge of the diner?' he says at last when Meg takes a breath and he has the chance to speak. At this point, it's the flight with Meg that he's worried about. He's pretty certain she's exceeded his acceptable limit of words (from other people) for the day, and it's only been about a half an hour since they met.

46

'After years of theorizing, I'm going to have to concede that when you know, you know, and you simply can't beat yourself up for what you didn't know when you didn't know it.' – Meg

Tania has had a long day. Turns out, making up with your long-time friend and business partner after a major future-threatening fallout and bringing each other up to speed on general life drama takes a whole workday. With some spillover saved for the next. This has all worked out splendidly though. This is what she wanted. It's the coming back home part and the anxiously checking phone every 30 seconds to see if Meg has called or texted part that she's not looking forward to. And it isn't helping that Nandu, Meenakshi Aunty and Muthu the watchman are betting on their bet (Nandu entirely on Tania's side, Muthu rooting for Meg and Meenakshi Aunty retiring to the fence) and are somehow always in the know on current developments.

But there is no anxiety that a long bath can't solve, she figures, and goes hunting through her drawers for all those scented candles and aromatic oils that she's been collecting in the hope of finding precisely this kind of time to enjoy the 'perfect bath'. Also, Meg's not home and she's the one with the fancy bathtub (which, of course, she uses as a sort of dumpster). Surely, she wouldn't mind Tania borrowing her tub. She is, after all, borrowing her Ryan at this very moment. Or at least that's how she feels. Tania quickly brushes the feeling aside, empties her bag of essential oil collection and tries to pick the ones that might work best for her at the moment. After three minutes, she decides on myrrh ('highly regarded in Biblical times and has an aroma that brings a deeper sense of spirituality') and ylang ylang ('a pure essential oil with a sensual and exotic fragrance that promotes inner peace, confidence and relaxation'). It takes her another 45 minutes to get done with the preparation – the mixing, scrubbing, massaging, finding the right music – and get to the good parts: sinking into the warmest bath ever, sipping cold lemon juice (because wine, contrary to popular belief, is really the worst thing for times like this) and leaving the world behind. But within 10 minutes of tub time, Tania is interrupted by the most irritating sound in the world: the doorbell. It's like some kid has found out that he can reach it and has decided to go to town with it. Whoever is at the door either really wants Tania to let them in, or they just really want to give her a migraine.

Infuriated, but more anxious than infuriated (what if it's an emergency?), Tania hurries out of the tub, tries to call out to whoever is at the door that she's on her way while towelling herself dry and trying to find something to get into. All she can find is the crazy chicken suit that she'd worn at the pre-school at Kodai and brought along with her for sentimental reasons. It's lying right there on Meg's bed where she had left it before going for her bath, having tried it on again to distract herself from 'Meg Ryan'. It's a bright yellow, somewhat inflatable, full-fledged chicken suit appropriate for a mascot for a chicken company.

Tania wants to unpack her suitcase and pull out something more sensible to wear instead, but the doorbell is relentless and by now, she's genuinely worried it's an emergency. 'Hang on, I'm coming!' she calls out and waddles towards the front door, her face being the only part of her body that's actually visible through the suit. She opens the door and finds a horrified Meg standing there.

'What are you doing here? And why have you been going at the doorbell like that? You have any idea how insane that was? You scared me!' The sight of Meg has temporarily made Tania forget that she's a chicken mascot standing at the doorway, calling people insane.

'Wow!' Meg says. 'The things people do when they're home alone.' And with that, she pulls Ryan, who has been hiding behind the wall, in front of her and yells 'Surprise!'

Once again, Meg is so caught up in her series finale, it hasn't occurred to her that Tania does not know a thing about what happened in Pune. Tania's heart slips out of her ribcage and drops straight into the pit of her stomach with a dull thud that can be heard through her chicken suit. She has, of course, immediately concluded that the two of them are now together. Though the very thought of that feels wrong. Even when they're standing right here in front of her. *Together!* Being 'Meg Ryan' and everything.

'Oh,' she says inarticulately. And a touch rudely, 'Ryan.'

Poor Ryan has had a bizarre day. This turgid chicken version of Tania is not helping matters one bit. He can't seem to think of anything to say. Meg watches the two of them for a couple of seconds and decides to drag them both inside the house and close the door. 'You guys clearly have some things to work out,' she says, leaving them standing in the living room in silence. 'Tania, you could start with the suit maybe? I have to go find Neel. I have grand feelings to declare,' she beams and proceeds to get changed into something a little more glamorous than jeans and a sweater.

Tania is lost. 'Neel? She's going to find Neel? What is she talking about?'

'Right,' Ryan finally gets over the chicken suit and remembers what he's here to do. 'The whole thing was a big misunderstanding,' he flounders. 'I don't even know where to start.'

'You can start with the dating app,' Tania says sharply.

'Yes, right. The app. Wasn't me.'

'But it sounded like you!'

'My sister. I'm sorry, she's difficult to explain. But she means well. This is not the first time she's tried to set me up, but I've got to hand it to her, this had the most insane consequences!'

'Butterfly effect,' Tania smiles through wet eyes.

Ryan pulls her close and tries to hug her, but the inflated chicken belly gets in the way. They laugh as Tania explains how she got into it and clarifies over and over that this isn't her weird fetish or anything.

'What the hell did you do in my bathroom?' Meg screams from inside. 'It smells like a witch's cauldron in here!'

Tania and Ryan laugh, and Tania can sense a significant talk coming. She desperately wishes she were wearing something else, but a chicken suit seems appropriate for a couple who've been taking turns to be chicken from day one.

'Listen,' Ryan says finally. 'I've been meaning to bring this up, but I didn't want to rush anything. And now that things have come to a head on their own, I suppose it's time I –'

'No, no, no, no! You listen.' Tania feels the need to stop what's coming. This is another romcom classic. The need to rush every plotline in the story when one reaches culmination. 'You don't have to say anything now. You've been hit with all this news all of a sudden, you've spent the entire flight with Meg –'

'Which was nuts, thank you for getting that!' Ryan admits.

'Yes, and Meg has had her big epiphany, and she's rushing over to Neel and it's all so wonderful and electrifying and magical. And just being around that energy can make you want to rush ahead too. And make a declaration of your own.'

Ryan is listening. She's right so far. This is exactly how he feels.

'I'm just saying, Meg and Neel are truly in their series finale. They've had the relationship, the break up, the back and forth, the doubts, the confusion, the trying other people out and the un-fightable pull back to each other. Trust me, if they drag this out any longer, the universe will retaliate with earthquakes and tsunamis. But you and I – we're in season one. And I'm fairly certain we won't need seven seasons to figure this out but there are many steps – baby steps, fun steps, adventurous steps – before we get to any kind of big declaration. You know?'

'Oh, I know. I was just going to clear up the app confusion and be on my way back. Why, what did you think was coming?'

Fuck, fuck, fuuuuuuck.

He waits five seconds for her to completely freak out and breaks into a smile. 'I meant, I'm happy to skip the speech if that's what you want,' and reaches out to kiss her. But the beak gets in the way of what should've been a moment. 'Oh, just get out of the damn suit!' Ryan says at last.

'But I'm also just a chicken standing in front of a boy…' Tania waddles into the room to get changed.

~

'Good luck out there,' Tania says, as Meg puts the finishing touches to her make-up and is all set to leave. 'Not that you need it.'

'You were right about this all along!' Meg is so overjoyed that she just might tear up and smudge her mascara. 'I can't believe you were actually right about something.'

'Aww,' Tania says. 'I know you mean that as a compliment.'

'Thank you for not giving up on us,' Meg says through weepy eyes.

'No, not now! You're going to smudge that mascara! Go get the guy already! I'll be right here for the post-euphoria analysis.'

'I love you!' Meg calls out as she rushes out the door and Tania smiles fondly like the mother hen – forgive the pun – that she's always been to Meg.

47

'I know it's about the journey, not the destination and all that, but that saying should come with a disclaimer that you can't quite appreciate the journey until you get to the finale.' – Tania

Meg looks stunning in her steel grey dress and red lipstick (a near middle-age experiment in cosmetic boldness) and she knows it. Her usually straight collarbone-length hair looks effortlessly elegant with just the right number of waves, a look that has taken her exactly 47 minutes to achieve. She's waited a long time for this episode of her life and it's been her perennial fear that the guy might end up doing the declaration, giving her no time to shower, let alone put together a look. But when she walks into Olive (the ridiculously overpriced restaurant Neel works at), she's told that he's at a fancy resort in the outskirts somewhere, shooting his TV debut. Meg makes a quick calculation: Wading through traffic to get to the resort will take her two hours. Time taken to put this special look together – 47 minutes. Look on Neel's face when she gives him the speech she's yet to prepare – totally worth it. When it comes to braving obstacles in the pursuit of true love, it's hard to keep a romcom enthusiast down (the enthusiast being Tania who seems to have infected Meg for the time being). Especially when effort and energy have gone into achieving a weirdly specific look in her head: *Like I've just walked out of a fancy schmancy office party. In New York. A party I've been waiting and preparing for for months, to meet an industry biggie who is about to open many doors for me. But I end up having this major revelation about my one true love when I'm in the ladies' room, and I must now choose between hanging around and befriending said industry biggie and running to the airport to stop my true love from taking that flight to Far-Far-Away Land. And I have chosen the airport.*

Her Uber arrives in less than a minute. It's an elegant sedan, though she asked for a small car (easier to wade through traffic). But she likes that the universe concurs with her 'big' theme this evening. 'Madam, how are you?' the driver greets her and Meg groans. Not a chatty driver. Not today! She has three speeches to deliver at three stopovers: an I'm-taking-life-into-my-own-hands-so-try-and-stop-me speech for her mother, a celebratory-slash-thank-you speech for Binny and of course, the grand declaration for Neel. A chatty driver is totally going to kill her thought process. She decides to focus on her speech and not make any eye contact with the driver through the rear-view mirror.

'Neel, we have to talk!' she says out loud.

'What, madam? You are saying something?' The driver, Muthu, smiles at her through the mirror. This isn't just a chatty driver, it's one who wants to impress her with his English, she notes. Which means more talking. Also, what's with the Muthus of Chennai hounding her! Just before she left, Watchman Muthu had insisted on giving her a three-minute pep talk on how she's totally going to win the bet. And now, this.

'No, no. I'm just practicing something, don't mind me,' she tells him. But now he's constantly making eye contact through the mirror and smiling every time he catches her eye. Meg wouldn't have been amused by this even on a regular day, but right now, it grates on every fibre of her being. This was not part of the script!

She tries telling herself this is like Katherine Heigl in 27 *Dresses* but it's really not. For starters, she'd never be able to change her clothes in the backseat of any running car in India, let alone a cab. She decides to focus once again and pictures herself bursting into Neel's office (he should be done with his shoot by then) and giving her speech. *What if Rebound Girl is around*, she suddenly wonders. She had forgotten all about her. She'd just have to listen to the speech too, she decides.

'Neel,' she starts again. 'I need to talk to you.'

'Yes, madam!' the driver beams.

'No, I'm not talking to you. I'm practicing a speech.'

'Oho. What speech, madam?'

Meg tries to be patient with the guy. He seems sweet and chirpy and she hates to ruin his evening by being snappy, but wisdom tells her that it's better to establish boundaries early on since this is going to be a long drive. 'Uh, it's nothing. Please, I need to practice. Can you not talk for some time?'

He looks hurt. Meg tries to ignore it but finds that she can't focus on the speech with the driver sulking. She groans in her head and decides to make the best of it. 'Okay. I'm going to tell someone that I love him. You have any ideas?'

'Oho! Wonderful, madam. Wonderful. Love is wonderful,' Muthu approves. 'Speak from heart, madam. That is how I spoke to my girlfriend.'

'Nice. What happened?'

'Oh, that is sad story, madam. Her father make her marry someone else.'

Oh god, Meg is screaming inside by now. She checks the app. She has another half hour to go.

'But after marriage, she is coming back to me.' Driver Muthu seems to have a whole other level of boundary issues, she notes.

'Okay,' Meg says. She's done indulging him. 'I really need to practice now.'

He's quiet for a few minutes. But Meg can't seem to do much more than rearrange the word order of her opening line. 'Fuck,' she says.

'Madam, no stress. Take my advice. Speak from heart means true love. Practice means no love.'

Meg is not sure if she wants to laugh or throw him out of the cab and take the wheel. But since her rehearsal isn't particularly working out, she decides to pull a Tania and take the cab driver's advice as 'a wink from the universe'. *Spontaneity* it is, she tells herself. *I just hope I don't miss any points.*

'Thank you,' she tells Muthu.

'True love wins,' he says and decides to unleash more of his pearls of wisdom at Meg for the rest of the ride.

'Stop, stop, stop!' she yells as they almost miss her mother's house. She jumps out of the car, quickly checks her watch and rushes in. She has about five minutes to deliver her speech and leave if she is to make it in time to see Neel. Thankfully, her mother gets to the door immediately.

'Meg!' Her mother sounds surprised more than disapproving, but Meg is on the defensive. 'Listen. Before you slam the door in my face –'

'You want to come in?' her mother says, worried that her daughter might be having that nervous breakdown everyone's been predicting.

'No, I don't have the time,' she says, entering the house anyway. Her mother carefully closes the door behind them so the neighbours don't hear whatever is about to come.

'I have been doing a lot of thinking and I just want you to know that while we may have bonded recently and though I may have let myself like it, I am not a child! You do not get to make me live your unlived life! That's just too much of a burden. And... I love Neel, and I'm on my way to go and tell him that. He has a job now and he's responsible even while being an artist. And you know what? I respect that. Hell, I love that. And I love him... yes, I love him...'

'Can I get you some water?' Now her mother's really anxious.

'No, you don't get to interrupt. I'm going to be with the person I love. This does not mean I'm making the same mistake you made. Neel is not my father.'

'I know tha–'

'I know that your life hasn't been easy,' Meg almost chokes out. 'But you really have to stop needing me to live the life you wanted...'

'I know,' Kavitha's voice is shaky too.

'And you believed that Rajeev Menon over me? That was not cool.' It's obvious from Meg's voice just how hurt she is.

Kavitha's eyes well up in response.

'That's about it. That's all I needed to tell you. Now I have to run!' Meg turns around in a hurry.

'So, see you next week for dinner? With Neel?' her mother says.

'Wow, I did not expect it to be this easy' Meg says under her breath.

'What?'

'I said yes,' Meg says turning around, smiling. 'Yes, we'll see you next week.'

'Okay, go, go, go!' She yells at Muthu. 'We're running late, and I have one more speech to deliver before THE speech.'

'Madam, if I'm going faster than this, police is catching us and no speech, no love only.' Meg groans but is thankful that Binny's office is on the way. They reach in 15 minutes.

'Great! You're doing nothing!' she says, barging into Binny's office.

'Meg…actually I was…' Binny tries to point out that she's now got more clients and is in the middle of making notes.

'You're not going to believe this, but I am on my way to claim my true love! And even better, I just stopped at my mom's place and told her exactly what I thought and…'

'Wait! You're going to talk to Neel?'

'Yes, obviously. Keep up! I don't have much time.'

'Okay, that's wonderful.' Binny is too shocked to react appropriately. 'Meg, why are you wasting time here? Go and see Neel!'

'Yes, but…'

'But what?'

'The way I'm feeling right now? Like I can do anything? What if I go there and find out that Neel has really moved on and doesn't want to be with me? Maybe I'll stop feeling so unstoppable then. So, I just wanted to let you know before that…that you have had everything to do with how I'm feeling now and where I am now. Even if this doesn't work out, I feel different. I'm a different person now. All thanks to you.'

Binny is so moved, she throws her arms around Meg, making her immediately regret making such an emotional speech.

'Okay, now I have to go,' Meg wiggles out of the hug.

'Okay,' Binny smiles through teary eyes. 'All the best! Go get him!' she screams as Meg runs in her heels through the corridors of Trinity Hospital and people start to stare disapprovingly at Binny.

~

'Madam! Good luck!' Muthu says as Meg gets off. 'Remember, no practicing!' Meg is at the venue 40 minutes earlier than she had initially calculated, a Virgo curse that she's grown accustomed to living with. Except tonight. More waiting time means more anxiety and if she's taking Muthu's advice and going the spontaneity route, she must just get this over with right now. She must find Neel wherever he is and just charge in, boldly declaring feelings, all consequences be damned. She walks over to the receptionist like a woman meaning business and enquires about the shoot. When the receptionist warily asks her who she is, she says co-producer without blinking. The steel grey dress and red lipstick work their magic, and the receptionist directs her to the room where the shoot is happening. She thanks her and takes purposeful strides in that general direction and once she's out of her line of sight, Meg starts to run in high heels like she's Erin Brockovich chasing after a new piece of evidence.

By now, the adrenaline has kicked in and Meg is wired to get her big movie ending, but what she isn't prepared for is that big movie endings demand taking on big potentially humiliating situations on the part of the person making the grand gesture. And when she dramatically throws open the doors of the hotel's ballroom screaming, 'Neel, I have to talk to you!' she isn't expecting:

a) To interrupt a show with a live audience
b) Cameras turning in her direction
c) A spotlight on her
d) General chaos

But if there's anything our heroine has learned from living with a woman who has spent more than two decades devouring the romcom genre, it's that you never chicken out in your series finale.

You stick it out through the humiliation, declare your feelings and kiss your beloved to thundering applause from the unsuspecting audience. The stakes have got to be high. That's when you know it's true love. Meg can hear her heart pounding in her ears, but it's too late to back down now. She has the attention of the entire room. And it's a large room.

'I'm crazy about you, Neel,' she begins. A collective gasp sweeps across the room. The audience is thrilled. This is a much better reality show than the one they signed up for. Meg, on the other hand, can barely see Neel. He's up on the stage and the lights are too blinding but she continues. 'I always have been. I was just too theory-driven to realize that you're perfect for me and that you always have been! You're my go-to person! Okay, Tania is my go-to person. But you're my other go-to person!'

At this point, two security guards start to escort her out of the room. 'Hey! Let go of me!' Meg is outraged. This isn't the way this was supposed to go. 'Do you people not understand romance?' she yells. And why wasn't Neel doing anything about it? 'Neel!' she screams as they nearly drag her out of the room.

'Let go of me!' Meg snaps at the security guard who is even more baffled than she is.

'Madam, you are fan of Harish sir *aah*?'

'What? What Harish? What fan?'

'Then why you tell Harish sir you love him?'

'WHAT?

At this point, Meg is led into what appears to be a conference room where the manager of the resort and one of the producers of the show Meg just disrupted, are waiting to get to the bottom of what just happened. She is clearly a gorgeous but rabid female fan that the show's producers have to deal with.

'Can someone please tell me what's going on?' Meg says seeing that the other two were too busy looking baffled to say anything.

'Uh…we were hoping that you would tell us,' the manager says. You can tell he's trying to sound like he's about to hand her over to the cops but he's failing, because never in all these years has he had to deal with a situation like this where the woman in question was sober.

Meg sighs. 'I need to speak to Neel. The one who's on that damn cooking show?'

'Cooking show….' they both say in unison. And finally something seems to click in their heads.

'Well share with me!' Meg is getting more and more impatient.

'The cooking show is at the other end of the floor. You were in a different show just now.' The producer says.

'A different show?'

'A quiz. But I assure you, we've never had the audience's attention as we did today. It was nice meeting you,' he looks amused but Meg is too confused and embarrassed to shake his hand so he leaves the room and rushes back to the show that… must go on.

'A…quiz? I just…said all that…to a room full of strangers…' Meg's face instantly turns hot and pink from embarrassment. The manager takes pity on her and kindly offers to bring Neel to her himself.

Two hours later, Meg and Neel are seated at a table in the 24-hour coffee shop. Neel can't stop laughing though his sides hurt and Meg is drowning her humiliation in a large mug of coffee, looking adorably cross. But the nice people at the quiz shoot have promised to send Neel the tape (of the grand declaration of feelings that he missed). Yes, the whole thing is now on tape.

That's not all. There is no Rebound Girl. The woman Suchi saw was Neel's cousin Priyanka, the only one in his extended family that he can actually tolerate. But Meg's finale is in every sense big and dramatic. She just wishes she could enjoy it someday.

'Shut up already!' she barks at Neel who's still laughing.

'This is why I love you,' he says, though she can't hear him through all the laughter and snaps at him all the way home. But it's going to take a lot more than snapping to make Neel angry anytime soon.

Epilogue: Three Years Later

Meg and Neel are married, and happily, by most people's standards, though Meg thinks there should be more written about life after happily-ever-after since that's really where the story begins.

Tania spends half the year with Ryan and Virus in Pune, two months with her mother in Kodai and the other four in Chennai with Ryan as well. They're making modern romance work for them. Ryan had insisted on being in Chennai with Tania but seeing how happy he was in Pune at the diner, Tania insisted on slicing the pie fairly. Ryan is very close to losing it with all the back and forth though, and is about to pop the big question to Tania, so they can just pick a city and live in it. Tania does not know this, but Meg and Neel are in on the plan.

Meg has finally started her own agency along with her former colleague Nitin from Red Dot. It's called Old School and STD – who has finally emerged from his post divorce-stress – is most proud of his favourite employee whom he's passed on many of his contacts to. What's more, Meg has completed her first novel and has just sent it out to various publishers. She doesn't want to make a big deal of it until something actually happens, but Tania and Neel are making this next to impossible. Neel almost announced on his show that his wife is going to be a bestselling novelist really soon.

Tania lives with Meg and Neel in their new apartment when she's in Chennai, though Meg's mother has made no secret of her disapproval on the grounds, 'What will people think?'

Tania and Aditi are well on their way to becoming one of the country's most sought-after wedding planners, thanks to Meera Anand's lifelong debt of gratitude to Tania for falling in love with her sister's fiancé.

Binny is back in Australia becoming 'a legit therapist' and still thinks fondly of her very first patient.

Meg and Tania continue to live happily ever after, now swapping theories for the sake of balance.

Acknowledgements

I didn't set out to write a book celebrating female friendship, but it did turn out that way, so a special shout-out to Andy, Divya, Chitra, Kirthi, Rhea, Nairy, Sudeshna, Madhu, Mai Vi, Hannah, Jo, Ola. Thank you for the unique space you occupy in my life. I love you.

Much love to my long-suffering daughter, who has been shushed many times for interrupting my thoughts in the making of this book and otherwise.

Grateful for my family, for their constant support through the roller coaster that is my life.

Special thanks to Samit for always having my back, and giving out the best career advice.

To my editor Niyati Dhuldhoya and the team at Hachette, thank you for catching everything I missed and making this book so much better than it would have been.